Echoes of Midnight

The Orion Dynasty Book 2

CK Franco

Blurbs

Lucien Blackwell is Manhattan's most feared attorney—cold, brilliant, untouchable. Mariel Dawson is a journalist chasing the Brotherhood's secrets, and Lucien is the story that could make or break her.

But obsession cuts both ways, and once she steps into his midnight, she may never find the light again.

Obsession. Betrayal. Desire that blurs the line between salvation and destruction.

To those who walk through the midnight hours with wounds the
world cannot see—
this story is for you.
May you find, in Lucien and Mariel's echoes, a reminder that even in
betrayal, grief, and silence, love has the audacity to rise.
For the dreamers who have been broken, and for the broken who dare
to dream again—
this book carries your heartbeat between its lines.

"The darkest truths echo the loudest,
but love—love is the one voice that refuses to be silenced."

Prologue

The courtroom lights burned like a stage where every gesture was judgment, every silence a verdict. Lucien Blackwell stood at its center—unflinching, immaculate, untouchable. To the world, he was power personified: the attorney who could bend the law without breaking it, the man who played midnight like a symphony of shadows.

But even gods of the gavel carry ghosts.

In the quiet hours when the city sleeps, Lucien hears them—echoes of promises unkept, of lives spared and shattered, of his own heart sealed in armor no one dares touch. Each victory is another brick in the fortress he's built to keep the world out... and himself caged within.

Mariel Dawson never planned to trespass into his silence. She only wanted truth, scribbled in ink and exposed in headlines. But truth is a dangerous seduction, and Lucien's midnight gaze carries both ruin and refuge.

What happens when the woman sworn to uncover him becomes the only one who sees him?

What happens when a man who vowed never to love finds himself breaking in her hands?

This is not just their story.

It is a collision of power and passion, betrayal and devotion— an echo that will not fade, even when the midnight is over.

Contents

Rain and Shadows in the City

Rain covers the city like a heavy blanket, making the streets wet and shiny. The water reflects the colorful lights from buildings and cars. Manhattan at midnight feels calm yet alive, with the soft sound of cabs passing by and distant laughter. Inside Mariel Dawson's apartment on the fourth floor, the atmosphere is very different. The corners of her room are filled with dark shadows, and the place is messy, with papers scattered everywhere. Old gray sofas hold piles of documents, many with bent edges and coffee stains, showing they've been there through many late nights of work. A single desk lamp casts a warm, soft glow, highlighting the clutter of her current investigation. Around the room, there are court papers, printed online posts with bright highlights, notebooks full of handwritten notes, and hand-drawn maps scattered about. Nearby, her tabby cat lies on the window ledge, flicking its tail now and then as traffic moves along Tenth Avenue.

Mariel sits right in the middle of this mess, cross-legged, with a worn notebook resting on her knee. Her fingers bear stains of ink and newspaper print, proof of how long she has been writing and researching. Outside, the city hums quietly like a busy hive, but inside, Mariel is alert. She smells the fresh rain on the streets and a faint aroma of burnt coffee. Behind her eyes, a dull ache tells her she hasn't had enough sleep. Every sound inside feels heavy and almost unreal. She pushes her tangled hair back and pulls the curtain wider to let in more light. The apartment feels like both a refuge and a cage—quiet outside but filled with a storm inside her mind.

A Notebook Full of Failures and Hope

Opening her notebook, Mariel sees pages covered with marks of failure. There are headlines quickly jotted down, notes about clues that led nowhere, and stories that never came to life. Names are circled and crossed out: a missing teacher, a business that closed without warning, rumors about a secret group called the "Brotherhood" that always seems to vanish when she gets close. These thoughts echo in her head like a voice from a phone call with Lauren, her editor.

Lauren's voice was sharp and tense when she said, "You're running out of time, Mariel. This isn't another wild goose chase. Give me facts, or someone else will. We both need this story."

The words hurt like a reminder of how fragile Lauren's trust is. The newspaper wants solid truth, not guesses. Mariel's will grows stronger. She has always dreamed of finding a big story that matters—one that could ease the pain from past betrayals. Years ago, a mentor took one of her stories and claimed it as their own. That betrayal still burns inside her. If she fails again now, she worries she will never be whole again—not in this city, not as a reporter.

Suddenly, lightning cuts across the sky, casting sharp shadows on the walls. Her phone, buried under the papers, starts buzzing with a strange vibration. Her heart speeds up as she grabs it and finds a message filled with strange numbers and letters. At first, they make no sense. But when she unlocks the code with a special app—something she learned to use during late nights with Ivy, a trusted friend—the message becomes clear.

A Warning and a Secret Message

The message warns her about deep corruption hiding offshore, illegal money transfers, and a group called Orion. It tells her to watch out and that danger is close. The warning gives her chills but also fire in her cheeks. She copies the critical details onto a sticky note, knowing this might be the real evidence she needs if she can follow the trail quickly enough.

Staring out the window at the city full of lights and hidden secrets, Mariel imagines powerful people moving in dark corners, their money and lies hidden behind expensive suits and locked doors. She thinks about how many times she has stood at this window, scared she might fail and have nothing to show for it. Her reflection stares back—hungry and restless. Breathing out, she makes a quiet promise to herself: this time, she will find the truth.

She pulls a yellow sticky note from the pad and writes, "Find the link—prove it," sticking it above her lamp. The small light feels like a guiding star. The room smells of rain and ink as her cat jumps down from the ledge, sensing the change.

Digging Deeper into the Mystery

Mariel returns to her desk and opens her laptop. Her screen fills with files containing names, money trails, and anonymous tips. She begins mapping out connections in her notebook, drawing arrows like spider legs stretching across the page. She whispers to herself, trying to piece everything together. Outside, a car horn blares, and thunder rolls, but she doesn't flinch. Fear is there, sharp and real, but her determination burns stronger. If this secret group controls the city, Mariel Dawson will shake its foundation.

Her eyes glance at the blinking phone again with the coded message. She reaches out and traces paths no one else wants to follow. Doubts cling to her skin, but she keeps pushing forward, ready for the challenge.

The Quiet of the Old Municipal Library

Morning finds Mariel stepping into the city's old municipal library. The heavy front doors creak as she enters the pale dawn filled with silence. Light filters through dirty windows, casting soft shapes on the worn marble floors. Flickering fluorescent bulbs struggle to banish the shadows in the corners. The air smells of dust and weathered paper. Her bag weighs heavily from piles of requested files and notes, making her shoulders stiff. She finds a quiet corner far from the city noise where peace takes over.

At her small wooden table, Mariel spreads out her materials: old case files tied with string, yellowed newspapers, and her laptop covered with fingerprints from long hours of work. Her pen, chewed nervously, hovers over a lined notebook. Here, details sharpen into clues and facts. Mariel feels both an observer and a hunter.

She opens the first folder, revealing news clippings and court reports. Certain names stand out—Lucien Blackwell, a defense lawyer who shows up often. Next to his name are mugshots and courtroom photos of men accused of crimes like murder and racketeering, which means running illegal businesses. Blackwell always wins these cases. Every victory seems like a trick that frees men who vanish after their trials.

The voice of her editor rings in her mind, asking for the bigger picture, the real reason for the story. Mariel pushes her doubts away and looks deeper. She reads the fine print of court decisions, hoping to find hidden links. She wonders why Blackwell defends these dangerous clients and why his wins open doors for secret companies and shady business deals.

Her eyes catch a surprising detail: some client names also appear in a leaked police file from an old detective. The file was released at midnight and then quickly hidden with threats and lawsuits. She pulls her laptop closer and carefully compares lists. The glowing screen brings focus to the tired lines on her face.

Mariel connects Blackwell's court wins to fake companies tied to the Orion Brotherhood. These companies mainly exist only on paper. They include charities and import-export firms with suspicious numbers. She draws lines in her notebook, creating webs of connections that spread across the page like a spider's trap. The dates line up perfectly with money moving through shell companies and real estate deals.

At the center is a clear pattern. Blackwell helps certain men win in court every time. These victories unlock flows of money into political campaigns and expensive properties. Mariel feels a metallic taste in her mouth—this is a machine of corruption.

Suddenly, she looks up, feeling nervous. The library is empty except for a custodian pushing a cart of old books. She senses invisible eyes watching from the shadows. In Manhattan, nothing stays hidden long. Courts are like stages where lawyers play roles in a world of blurred morals. Powerful people write scripts behind closed doors, hiding their crimes under the law. Mariel wonders how many webs like this might exist and who else might be watching her.

Her hands shake as she review her notes. Is this all too wild? But the pattern is there, as real as the city's pollution. She feels a mix of fear and awe—for Blackwell, the corruption, and the scale of it all. And she feels very alone in this chase.

Memories flash back of a source who betrayed her once, almost ruining her career. Trust is rare, but now more than ever, she wants someone to believe in her. She whispers to herself, wondering if she is chasing shadows.

A librarian returns, moving silently among the shelves. Mariel leans back, exhausted, and flips through a faded news clipping showing Blackwell's shadowy face. Her hands tremble as she closes the notebook, as if shutting a door on dark secrets.

"This is bigger than I thought," she says softly.

The Newsroom and the Big Meeting

Daylight pours through the glass and steel of The City Herald's newsroom. Lauren Cassidy's office sits above the noise. It's a glass room filled with sunlight and the distant sound of the city. Mariel places her hands on Lauren's polished desk and opens her notebook filled with diagrams linking the Orion Brotherhood to Blackwell and his clients.

Lauren studies the notes quietly, her expression serious. She's dressed sharply in a pale blue suit, tapping her finger on a legal pad. Outside, the newsroom buzzes with phones ringing and printers whirring, but inside it's still. Mariel breaks the quiet with energy.

"The corruption isn't just a surface thing," she says. "It's a system tied to Blackwell. When you connect fake companies to his court wins and follow the money, it always circles back. Someone is using the courts to clean dirty money."

Lauren raises her eyebrows. "Be careful, Mariel. Your story sounds exciting, but right now it's just a theory. You have a lot of coincidences and strong feelings. Blackwell and his allies are dangerous. They don't like reporters digging around."

"That's why I have to keep going," Mariel says softly. "No one else will uncover this. Give me two weeks. I'll look into political donor lists and property deals. I won't stop."

Lauren's eyes harden. "Walking away might be safer—for your career and safety. I need proof, not guesses. I won't lose another reporter over something we can't print."

"I won't fail," Mariel promises, even though fear tightens her chest. The office feels cold and serious, leaving no room for doubts or dreams.

Lauren nods sharply and returns to her notes, sending Mariel back to the noisy newsroom below.

Mariel steps into the busy hallway, feeling the city's pulse fade behind her. Lights hum overhead as she pulls out her phone, her hands shaking. Taking a deep breath, she calls Natalia.

"Natalia, check political donor lists for anything odd. Look for offshore accounts, fake names—anything linked to Blackwell's clients. I want a report tonight."

Natalia's voice is steady but worried. "Are you taking on too much?"

"Maybe. But I have to follow this," Mariel says and hangs up. Then she dials Ivy.

"Ivy, can you review the flagged emails from the tip line? There might be money laundering or worse. It's all connected to Blackwell and those fake companies."

Ivy answers quickly, teasing but serious. "A digital rabbit hole? I'm already there. Stay safe. The people you're messing with hate attention."

As evening falls, the office glows amber with the sunset. Lauren's warning echoes in Mariel's mind as she leaves. She climbs the stairs to her building's rooftop, each step steady on rough concrete, her breath even against old wounds.

Outside, the city stretches below, bright and restless. A cold wind carries smells of rain and smoke. Footsteps fade into silence. Alone, Mariel holds her phone tightly and listens to the hum of the city that never sleeps.

Memories of betrayal come back—how her first big story was stolen, nearly ruining her career. Those dark times made her cautious. Every dead end, every threat chipped away at her sense of safety, leaving behind a hunger that drives her now.

Lauren's caution rings in her ears, filled with warnings of lawsuits and lost stories. She thinks of Natalia's loyalty, Ivy's skill, and how rare trust is. But now she knows this is the story she must chase, no matter what.

Wrapping her arms against the cold, her eyes sting as she looks east toward the city's glowing towers. Secrets here last longer than the people hiding them.

She breathes out quietly, "No matter the cost. I will finish this."

The Fixer's Domain

The skyscrapers of Manhattan stare down at Lucien Blackwell like sentinels, their glass eyes glinting with secrets borrowed from every law, every lie, and every bargain ever made in the shadows. Within the transparent box of his corner office, Lucien sits at a mahogany desk lacquered to a near-black shine, its surface blanketed with files—white-gloved with fingerprints, the stale scent of toner and coffee clinging to their edges. Court documents gleam on glowing monitors, their lines of text forming a code only the ruthless could truly decipher. His pen arcs across legal motions in a steady, merciless rhythm, slashing through prosecution claims—an executioner's hand disguised as a scholar's. The city outside offers no comfort; neon flickers against the window, reflected in Lucien's steel-cut eyes—an event horizon to everything he is sworn to shield and devour.

In this world, victories are currency. Spectacle is as essential as proof, and trials become theater for the hungry crowds—reporters, politicians, power brokers—united in their devotion to the spectacle, their devotion to the mask. Judges, attorneys, and clients bend to unspoken codes; words and evidence are weapons, but influence is the force that moves destinies behind glass and marble. Manhattan's legal heart beats not in the pursuit of justice, but in the snaking passageways where organizations like the Orion Brotherhood turn verdicts into lifelines for their empire, cloaking crimes in the language of reason and law. Lucien's preparations are surgical, layered, relentless: any missed flaw in the evidence is an unbarred door, an invitation for ruin—one miscalculation, and the Brotherhood's centuries-old roots could rot in the glare of ordinary justice.

Lucien's noteless mind hums with a thousand scenarios, each one an answer to a threat not yet spoken. Every margin in his leather-bound notebook traces the collapse of a prosecution argument; every Post-it flag marks not just a detail, but the weight of a life—his, his client's, the traitor's—hanging by a frayed silk thread. His jaw aches with repressed tension as his immaculate fingers pause over a damning photograph, a crime scene squalid with loss, another soul damned or saved depending on which way the scales will tilt. In the cold hush before dawn, Lucien rehearses—statute, precedent, deception, deflection—each rehearsal a shield against failure, each breath a negotiation between conscience and duty.

When he finally leaves the oasis of strategy, the pulse of the city buzzes in the marrow of his bones. Lucien's footsteps echo unresolved across the polished marble of the lobby before disappearing into the alley behind Blackwell & Kane—an artery where the city's lifeblood runs darker. There stands Marcus Reed, shoulders cloaked in a darkness deeper than the late morning gloom, eyes wary and unreadable, the Brotherhood's mark etched in muscle and stance.

"You know what's at stake, Lucien," Marcus murmurs, the air between them bitten with rain-slick chill and the bite of musty tobacco drifting from a distant dumpster. "This isn't just another body on trial. You lose, you crack the door. Their lights shine into all our corners."

Lucien's own voice—the controlled edge of a blade, polite, unyielding—carries none of the sleep-starved tremor beneath his skin. "No door opens today. I have every angle covered."

"Every angle, Blackwell? Even the ones we don't see until it's too late?" Marcus shifts, boots scraping wet brick, a silhouette carved out of warning and loyalty laced with dread.

"I'm not in the habit of inviting chaos, Marcus. I'll keep our house silent." His gaze never wavers, though inside, Lucien courts the ghost of hesitation—Brotherhood survival or personal damnation? As they part, the city's noise surges—a car backfires, glass shatters in the alley's far end—and Lucien is already building new contingencies in his mind.

He emerges in the brutal light of the courtroom. Baroque plaster arches loom overhead, the hush electric as the trial begins. Reporters poised with notebooks, eyes gleaming, record every raised objection, every tick of the judge's brow. Lucien, in a sapphire suit tailored to military precision, stands unyielding at the defense table. His voice slices through ambiguity—objection, hearsay, speculation—turning the prosecution's evidence back upon itself with a surgeon's dexterity. He exposes contradictions, timing statements to the subtle shifts in jury posture and the glint in the judge's narrowed eyes, as if reading the very currents that move the room. Across the well, the opposing counsel sweats, stumbles, papers trembling—all the performance of justice, but Lucien writes the script.

The gallery watches, verdicts whispered in secret—Brotherhood loyalists in the last row, faces expressionless but eyes hungry for assurance that the world they own beneath the city's skin will not bleed out into public daylight. Above them, the judge hands down the ruling with a slow, deliberate weight.

"In favor of the defense," she intones, her gavel thudding like thunder through a space grown suddenly brittle with consequence.

Lucien gathers files with a magician's sleight, not a hint of triumph touching his elegant features. Relief is forbidden. Eyes lock as photographers' flashes strobe the courtroom, capturing shadows where victory feeds on silence and not on jubilation. The prosecution wilts, packing up defeat; the Brotherhood's secret survives another day.

Lucien moves toward the door, the measured stride of a man who leaves nothing—and no one—unaccounted for. His own reflection flickers like an omen on the polished marble, fractured and whole, and the world outside awaits, as ravenous as ever.

Lucien emerges from the courthouse, shoulders rigid beneath the weight of his tailored coat. Evening clings to him—humid, electrical—while neon lights flicker above the city's veins, casting a chemical glow across rain-streaked pavement. The air is still and taut, buzzing faintly with the residue of legal spectacle. Near the curb, the Brotherhood's black sedan idles, glistening with new rain. The private driver's face is unreadable in the dimness, eyes shadowed by the brim of his cap. A silent nod, and Lucien slips inside.

The ride is soundless save for the faint hum of the engine and his own breath, which slows and thickens as Manhattan blurs by outside, a current of lights and secrets. Buildings flicker past, each window burning with private dramas and ambitions not so different from the world he inhabits—except most of those stories end with far less blood and consequence. He closes his eyes, but the day's echoes tumble in: the hollow thud of the judge's gavel, the stifled sobs of a woman in the gallery, the iron tang of adrenaline on his tongue as he dismantled the prosecution with surgical precision.

At the Orion Club's discreet side entrance, two guards appear from shadow, badges of velvet and steel signifying a sanctuary for the chosen, for those whose sins are sanctioned by power. Lucien is ushered down a private corridor awash in muted golds and midnight blue. He leaves behind the low pulse of the main bar, entering a lounge padded with velvet so deep it swallows footsteps. He crumples into a leather armchair set beneath a heavy velvet drape. For a moment, the air is thick with the scent of tobacco, whiskey, and secrets—he lets his head fall forward, elbows to knees, a solitary figure balancing victory atop a scaffold of invisible ruination.

He pours an inch of whiskey from a crystal decanter, the amber liquid fracturing lamplight across the grain of his hand. The glass is cold, the whiskey's burn bright but brief. He holds it aloft, peering through the swirl as if the depths of the glass might reveal something purer than memory. Instead, images: blood-dark crime scene photos splayed on courtroom screens, the pleading eyes of a mother whose child would never return, the slow, controlled breathing of the man he defended—guilt pooling in the silence between words. Each crafted objection, each carefully twisted narrative, has buried someone else's truth. His jaw tenses—pain lacing through flesh and bone—as he weighs the currency of survival: whose stories are erased, whose lives are splintered, so the Brotherhood's empire persists another day.

The door opens with a whisper of hinges. Elias Kane enters, his step confident and composed, the shadow of command preceding him. He closes the door and sits across from Lucien, hands folded, gaze sharp as winter glass.

"You look as if you've swallowed poison," Elias says, his voice pitched low, tone more verdict than observation.

"A symptom of the job," Lucien replies, his words measured, suffused with tired precision.

"Ignoring poison doesn't make you immune," Elias counters. His eyes cut through the haze between them, seeing beneath the polished surface to the hairline fractures webbing Lucien's resolve. "You delivered well today. But there's a toll, Lucien. Slippery lines—right, wrong. One day you'll find they're dust," he warns, his voice weighted with the iron certainty of experience. "Do you remember why you started down this path?"

Lucien's silence is loud. The question hangs in the thick air, its edges pricking the last shelter of his composure.

"For the Brotherhood. For survival. For—" He stops, the usual answers suddenly hollow.

"For yourself?" Elias's mouth is a thin, wry line. "Or for something else you no longer trust?"

Lucien looks away, heat prickling beneath his collar. The city's lights bleed through the curtain, painting the rug in restless patterns. He replays the day: the prosecution's faces as his arguments sliced their case apart, the subtle nods of Brotherhood loyalists in the back row, the gavel's finality. Whose protection mattered? The Brotherhood's, always first—and yet, a procession of lost faces haunts him, slipping behind his eyelids in relentless procession.

If he abandoned this path—could he unearth his old self, the one who believed in fairness, in law rather than its manipulation? He imagines it for a flicker: a life less burdened, a city where he is not a shadow's hand. But the vision collapses beneath the gravity of what has been done and what loyalty demands. Redemption seems like an artifact from another world, irretrievable.

Elias studies him, a chessmaster parsing an opponent's feint.

"Loss reminds us we're human," he says, the words as gentle as they are scathing. "But survival—Brotherhood—demands forgetting."

The club's clock ticks, relentless and soft.

Lucien straightens, running his thumb along the edge of his polished cufflinks as if assembling a mask from muscle and silk. He leaves the unfinished whiskey on the table, the ghost of his reflection fractured in amber. He repeats to himself, silent, as he stands: Brotherhood survival comes first. Brotherhood survival, always.

He crosses the lounge, pauses for a heartbeat at the threshold, then vanishes into the corridor, letting the door hush shut on Elias's warning and the remnants of his doubt.

Lucien crosses the threshold into the Orion Club's deep belly, the hush of midnight velvet pressing close. The corridor ahead glows with the soft promise of privilege—each step muffled by Persian rugs, his shadow bending along paneled walls where candlelight flickers in ornate sconces. The air is cut with old whiskey, expensive cologne, and the ghosts of a thousand whispered secrets. Past midnight-blue drapes shrouding tall windows lies the city, blurred and untouchable. As Lucien moves, club regulars eye him with the measured calculation that comes with survival in this world: judicial robes loosened over whiskey, cufflinks flashing with political insignia, silver hair bowed in quiet collusion. Their conversations splinter and shift as he passes, voices dropping, hands stilled over crystal tumblers—each nod a subtle exchange, the code of those who know their fortunes shape and are shaped by the man in the tailored suit. Trust here is a currency, parceled out in increments gleaned from past trials, old betrayals, and bargains brokered in the hush between verdicts.

The bar anchors the club, black marble slick beneath his palm. To Lucien's left, two power-suited businessmen murmur over the delicate fate of a campaign: cash filtered through shell foundations, assurances barely veiled. Their words brush backgrounds of newsprint scandals and midnight meetings, rehearsing scripted denials for the day the city calls in its debts. On his right, a former police commissioner shifts closer to his circle, cheap victory bristling in his tone—a favor delivered, an inconvenient file conveniently misplaced, the Club's reach lengthening under the table. Lucien tunes his senses to the rhythm of these exchanges: the careful pauses, the rye prompts, the practiced laughter that rings hollow where real danger waits. The club around him exhales power, its walls heavy with secrets accumulated through years of bargains and betrayals, the memory of trials where Lucien carved victory from ruin and rewarded loyalty with silence.

A soft pulse vibrates in his pocket. Lucien draws the slim communicator—numbers only, a signal. He threads past a mosaic of hushed intrigue and ducked glances into a book-lined antechamber where a hidden door swings open at his approach. Inside, pale light pools over a round table; Elias Kane sits at its heart, statuesque, his gaze fathomless and cold. At his left, Marcus Reed leans forward, hands folded, a line drawn tight between deference and tension. Three senior advisors—one a bony banking mogul, another an oily media strategist, the third a judge whose verdicts have saved more than one Brotherhood neck—complete the crescent. A dossier splits the table, bleeding recent intelligence: screen-grabbed headlines, internal memos stained with paranoia, names circled in red where rival empires threaten the Club's supremacy.

"The City Herald's inquiry is tightening around the Lovato deal," the judge states, voice razor-thin.

Elias's eyes glint. "They have a scent, but not a confession. Yet."

Marcus's jaw flexes. "We move the witness out tonight. No one will find her unless we want her found."

Lucien glances at the streaks of crimson ink slashed through the pages. Beneath each line, he recalls past nights: silencing a leak in time to save their accounts, losing an ally whose betrayal cost them half a council seat. The memory of those fractures lives in his bones—a calculus of trust and threat, equilibrium forever at the brink. Alliances are forged and broken here in equal measure; forgiveness is a myth no one truly believes.

"Our enemies grow bolder," murmurs the banker, fingering his signet ring. "Vega's contacts fed disinformation to the Tribune. Even Drake's investments wobble under scrutiny."

Lucien's voice, even and cool: "Then we double down. We keep our house airtight or the rivals cut our throats in the street." Each word wells up from scar tissue—the learned caution of a man who has gambled everything, won more than his share, and lost just enough to know fate's taste.

Elias regards him with a measure of pride and something sharper. "What's your play, Lucien? We can't weather another scandal if Dawson digs deeper."

Lucien meets the man's stare, unblinking. "Contain the story. Control all doors in and out. No one outside the room learns what we own. If we need to burn a name, we do it before breakfast."

A silence sits in the room, weighted—a pact made and tested countless times.

The council disperses on soft footsteps, their promises and warnings trailing in the charged air. Lucien drifts to the far wall, drawn to the window that overlooks a Manhattan awash in neon and shadow. The city gleams, invincible from this height, yet in the glass, he sees his own face ghosted—sharp, tense, eyes rimmed with exhaustion he won't allow. Behind him, the club pulses: deals struck by men who've survived the cost of loyalty, haunted by fractures that never fully mend. He knows them all by the friction in their greetings, by the guarded warmth of their trust. Here, any moment silence can become a weapon.

He thinks of Mariel—her investigation, the risk of exposure. He calculates the ache lodged in his chest as the price for devotion to something built on secrets. He balances pride in the empire he shields against the dread of unraveling; every privilege he preserves is stitched to fragility. Exhaustion presses at the edge of his vision. Yet he hardens his resolve in the hush, eyes fixed on the swarming web of city lights.

In the shimmering dark, Lucien makes his vow: whatever comes, he will stand at the threshold, sword drawn, the boundary between empire and oblivion.

Behind him, the club's doors close on the night's conspiracies; ahead, the city waits, restless—ready for the next gambit.

The Ballroom in Golden Light

Golden light spreads across the entrance of the Halloway, shining brightly on the polished marble pillars and the crystal doors. These pillars stand tall and smooth, reflecting the warm glow and creating a welcoming effect. The crystal doors catch the light, making their edges shine and sparkle. Outside, guests leave the cold night behind to enter the ballroom. Their rich clothes and elegant appearances are highlighted by the bright lighting, adding to the feeling of luxury. Small details, like cufflinks, glitter like tiny stars on men's shirts, while women's silk gowns flow softly as they move. The gentle scent of perfume follows the women, mixing with the crisp air. Around the room, laughter sounds clear and sharp, almost like the clinking of coins, adding to the lively atmosphere.

Mariel is part of this scene, moving through the crowd calmly and efficiently. She wears a simple black dress, carefully chosen for its purpose rather than style. Hidden at her side are a camera and a recorder, tools she needs for her work. Inside, everything looks perfect, as if untouched by any troubles. Champagne glasses are stacked high in towers under sparkling chandeliers that scatter light everywhere. Servants, dressed neatly in uniforms embroidered with gold thread, move quietly between groups of powerful guests. Every color of dress and every smile seems to hide secrets, giving the room a hidden tension beneath its beauty.

The City's Power in the Room

The ballroom is full of the city's real power. Important people speak in low voices or use secret codes so that no one outside the group understands. The heirs to big hedge funds shake hands with judges and city officials, making deals and forming alliances. Their eyes constantly move, watching for friendly faces and warning signs of danger. Mariel feels the tension beneath the excitement, a feeling that is sharp and strong. She knows the Orion Brotherhood is here; sometimes they show themselves openly, and at other times they hide in the shadows. Their influence is woven into every laugh and toast, invisible but very real. It is like a pull that connects everyone beneath the music and fun.

Lucien Blackwell's Arrival

When Lucien Blackwell arrives, everything changes. A black town car stops outside, and he steps out, his coat moving as he walks confidently through the glass entrance. Mariel's breath catches. She has studied his photos many times, but seeing him in person makes him seem even more dangerous and controlled than she expected. A small scar on his jaw catches attention more than any of the news stories she has read about him. She holds her camera tighter. At this moment, her investigation stops being just a secret plan and becomes very real.

Lucien moves around the room, passing groups of investors and socialites laughing and wearing diamonds. Mariel blends into the crowd, moving like a shadow among the rich guests. Even though her hands shake slightly, her fingers stay steady as she quietly raises her camera and takes pictures of him in conversation. Lucien smiles smoothly, showing no sign of worry. But when he turns away from a senator, his eyes scan the room carefully. He is aware that someone is watching him.

The Confrontation

Mariel moves toward the buffet table, where candles shine next to plates of salmon and bright fruit. She lowers her camera, but from across the hall, Lucien meets her gaze. His look is calm but sharp, as if he is studying evidence on a table. Slowly, he walks toward her, blocking her way to a hallway. His smile is cool and a little amused. "Looking for a story, Ms. Dawson?" he asks softly, his voice carrying an edge of danger.

The feel of the ballroom changes. A violinist suddenly misses a beat, and the nearby laughter becomes cold. Mariel steadies herself despite feeling fragile inside. "I'm looking for facts," she says clearly, meeting his eyes. "That's more than you can say when you defend men who hide the truth and hurt the victims." She holds her camera like a shield. "Who protects the people who suffer while you cover it up?"

Lucien's smile sharpens and becomes icy. "Justice isn't simple," he says. "It's full of mistakes and deals made behind the scenes. I follow the rules. Your anger should be aimed at those who write those rules, not the ones who play by them."

Mariel doesn't back down. "You make the system work for the worst people. How many times has your courtroom act helped someone escape and hurt others who couldn't afford your kind of defense?"

"That's rich," he replies, his eyes hardening. "Since when do journalists care about the damage done? How many people have you ruined with one careless headline, Mariel?" His voice grows tense, as if hiding a deep hurt.

People nearby quiet down, watching the intense exchange. The party's shine starts to feel fragile. Mariel senses Lucien's focus on her, his look filled with judgment and something more complex, as if he is trying to figure out what she really is.

Her voice is steady. "I don't make up evil stories just to sell news. You—"

"But you never miss a chance to make yourself the hero," he cuts in, eyes locked on hers. "You chase the smell of blood as much as the truth."

Mariel meets his gaze without blinking. His expression changes slightly, melting anger, respect, and curiosity together.

Their words stop, leaving only tension between them. The noise of the city presses against the ballroom windows, but here, the air feels charged and alive. Mariel breathes deeply, feeling the space between them both wide and thin. Lucien studies her, as if trying to stop an explosion about to happen.

Finally, his voice softens but remains firm. "If you want to challenge the devil, do it where you won't become a show for others. Shall we?"

He gestures to a door leading to a balcony lit by moonlight. Mariel does not hesitate. Her jaw tight, she moves with him from the gold-lit room into the cool night. The city's elite watch them, blind to the real battle taking place.

The Balcony's Truth

Lucien leads Mariel through heavy velvet curtains and onto the cool night balcony. The marble curves above the glowing city, slick from earlier rain and filled with hidden secrets. He stops and looks at the bright skyline but seems divided—focused on the midnight city and the restless pulse beside him. Glass towers reach up, their lights forming a map in the dark grids below. Lucien rests his hands on the stone railing, calm but holding memories and purpose. To those who do not know him well, he seems casual, but there is more inside him.

Mariel steps closer in the moonlight. The scent of the party fades—no more roses, bourbon, or caviar. Now the air smells sharp and metallic, like the city itself. Lucien notices her alertness, breaking through his usual calm. Her shoes make soft sounds on the marble, a small but determined act against the music fading behind them. She stands near him, holding the recorder tightly, her lips set in a firm line.

She speaks, her voice low and steady, edged with anger. "How many monsters have you protected, Blackwell? How many stories have you hidden behind your defense and your Brotherhood's power?" She does not raise the recorder, but her words hang in the air, supported by the fire in her eyes. "You say the law defends you, but who protects the victims when verdicts are bought?"

For a moment, Lucien drops his mask. Her words hit deeper than she thought they would. Inside, he feels a pain in the empty places where his conscience lives. He has spent years telling himself the law is a weapon and secrecy is a duty. Now her questions feel like stones hitting glass—testing it, maybe cracking it. His face tightens, and his breath changes for a second.

"Do you think the world is so simple?" His tone stays steady but carries hidden pain. "Victim, villain, truth—they mix together, Mariel. The system crushes everyone. I make the hard calls no one else will because in this world, you do what's needed or get crushed."

His words come from a cold, old place inside him. His eyes stay on the city, but Mariel's strong belief shakes his thoughts. The lines blur: one side trusting poison and violence, the other standing here now with anger and integrity.

She studies his face. The small scar on his jaw stands out in the city light. The shield breaks. "What about you?" she asks quietly, her voice fragile and soft with something unexpected. "When you chase justice or try to run from it—you start to lose track. Truth isn't always enough." A shake in her voice cuts through his confidence. "Sometimes I'm scared I'll become the corruption I'm fighting."

Her honesty catches him off guard. Lucien blinks, unsteady. He sees more than an enemy here; he sees a woman whose fierce spirit is tied to fear and a desperate need to clean the city's rot. Suddenly, he is unsure what role he plays: judge, protector, or something more dangerous.

He steps closer, closing some space between them—a test neither wants to give up. "That's your gift and your curse," he says quietly, a voice caught between warning and respect. "You chase hope like money, but you risk burning out." The night air feels charged, alive like the city's neon lights.

She does not back down. "Someone must believe change can happen, Lucien. That shining a light still matters. Without that, all we have left is giving up."

He shakes his head, a dry smile on his face. "Hope won't help you when people like me—like the Brotherhood—change the rules as they want. You fight ghosts. I fight the real people controlling them."

"In that case, you're just as trapped as I am. All your moves and power—do they change anything except the names on the doors?" Her words are full of iron and desperation. Lucien falls silent, realizing her broken but stubborn faith stirs a longing in him he hides every night. Their stalemate feels like an old spell, dangerous and full of possibility.

For a while, silence rules. Mariel looks past him to the city's uncertain future. Lucien watches her—the woman who might destroy his world and his silence. The tension between them is old and new, strange but familiar.

At last, he speaks, his voice heavy with warning and something neither wants to say. "Be careful, Mariel. You're deeper in this than you realize." He stares at her, searching for certainty but finding none. Then he steps back into the dark. Mariel stays, heart pounding, the glowing city holding all the threats and hopes their meeting has created.

Night in Manhattan

Puddles on the cracked pavement catch the flickering pink light from a broken neon sign. The faint glow spills onto graffiti-covered bricks, where rough images of wolves fade in the damp. The city feels different now. Gone is the bright, busy daytime bustle. At night, Manhattan turns wild, with narrow alleys filled with broken glass and deep shadows. Thick secrets hang in the cold, moist air. On West 41st Street, the usual city noises fade away. Distant headlights pass quietly, a siren wails far off between tall buildings, and a tense feeling presses on anyone who walks here.

Mariel moves through the alleys with care. She walks quietly and lightly on the slippery concrete, careful not to make any sudden noise. Her old jacket is tight around the camera hanging on her chest, ready to capture anything important. Each breath she takes turns into a small cloud of mist in the cold air, only to fade away quickly. She knows the Brotherhood controls this part of the city at night. Their presence feels heavy in every dark corner, like a warning to keep away. Dirt sticks to her skin, and the wind carries strange smells—old fried food from a closed shop and cold rainwater running through the gutters.

Ahead of her, under a yellowing sign flickering weakly, the old Club Nebula stands quiet. Two men stand near a service door covered in graffiti. Their jackets have silver stars and circles, the signs of the Brotherhood. Though their faces are hidden in shadows, their tense stances show they are alert and ready. They watch carefully, like trained soldiers guarding a secret.

A third man steps out from the darkness. He's sharply dressed, his face half-lit purple by a nearby light. He quietly hands over a briefcase to one of the men. Mariel presses herself against a cold metal trash bin, her heart racing. Her thumb hovers over the camera button, ready to snap pictures before she is caught.

She lifts her phone above a cracked trash bin. Every tiny movement is risky—if someone looks her way, if a light flashes suddenly, if her angle is wrong. But her hand is steady. The gleam on the briefcase, the Brotherhood's symbol on the jacket, the tilt of a chin—all captured in blurry but clear images that could prove everything. This is what power looks like at night. Mariel writes down the time, symbols, and a license plate—6FG 1142—in her soaked notebook. The ink blurs from a raindrop, but the adrenaline sharpens every detail. Nearby, a luxury town car waits silently at the alley's edge, shining in the decay. It will carry the deal's planner deep into Manhattan's veins.

Business in Manhattan at night relies on moments like this. Secret deals hidden beneath rain and forgotten streets, controlled by the Brotherhood. They are not just rumors. They are real, running arms deals, making judgments, silencing witnesses, and buying justice. The city's steel supports skyscrapers above but acts like invisible prison bars underground. Above ground, billboards and bright lights fade into the distance. Below, kings rule quietly in graffiti-covered corners.

Justice is bought and sold in dark cases with whispered passwords shared by men whose gloves hide decades of scars from brutal fights. Mariel is both intruder and witness here, feeling the city's hidden truths deep inside.

She crouches down again, pressing her notebook between her knees. Fear and hope mix up her spine like cold and fire. Her instincts scream to run, to hide, to disappear. But her need to learn the truth and reveal it is stronger than her fear. Past betrayals linger in her mind. People she trusted once stayed silent when it mattered, and teachers gave up on her dreams. What she discovers tonight may never save her or see the light, but she will not stop. Her fear will not become the burden she carries home.

Her fingers shake as she sends an encrypted message to Natalia and Ivy. She holds her breath until it is fully sent. Her words break into small parts: West 41st, Club Nebula, Brotherhood deal, briefcase, town car 6FG 1142, sending photos. For a moment, her courage feels as fragile as the mist that glows weakly in the streetlight. Then quietly, she deletes everything to keep herself safe.

The phone screen flickers once, then goes dark. Mariel presses back against the wall, tense and watchful. Footsteps sound nearby. She can't tell if it's just the wind or something worse.

She slips into a narrow path between scaffolding and old stone walls. She grips her camera and notebook tightly as darkness closes behind her. The city's heart beats louder here, mixed with oil, blood, power, and secrets. Mariel becomes part of this living web, driven by a strong will. With proof in her hands, she moves deeper underground, just another shadow carrying truths that only the brave seek.

Quiet in Hell's Kitchen

Far from the rain-soaked alleys, Hell's Kitchen glows quietly between midnight and the early morning hours. Natalia Voss sits at a smooth marble bar, the bass of faint music humming beneath her feet. Her fingers lightly tap the stem of a glass, cold and wet in her hand but untouched. She keeps her eyes low, watching the shiny ring on the bartender's finger. It is not a token of friendship but a sign of careful meetings and a cautious understanding.

The bartender waits for her to speak. He stands near private booths where Gotham's secrets mix with expensive drinks. Natalia leans in slightly, her voice soft and calm, careful not to reveal any worry.

"Quiet night. Any new faces around?" she asks, barely louder than the ice clinking and distant laughter.

He wipes a glass without looking up. "Security's tighter these nights. Brothers don't drink much when working." He glances at her and seems to read her unease. "Lucien's people brought two men I don't know. One has a gold star on black. The other moves with the quiet strength of a lion in someone else's den." His voice warns of danger. "Someone asked about you and Dawson too."

Natalia feels her heart race. Memories flood back of times when she and Mariel risked everything together. Now, the danger feels darker and closer. The bartender's words stir painful memories of friends who turned into enemies and times when trust was broken. She tastes the bitter memory as if it were on her tongue—the price of trusting the wrong person. Betrayal smells like sweat and storm, changing the look in a stranger's eyes.

Her bond with Mariel, built through years of work at the Herald and near misses, holds her steady. She chooses her words carefully, circling back to Mariel's safety. It is not just about gathering information. It is about protecting their family's legacy of never giving in to fear.

"Have you noticed any other changes at the usual spots?" Natalia asks, her voice soft but her eyes sharp. "Are the Brotherhood nervous?"

The bartender shrugs. "Meetings moved to hidden places now. Kane keeps watch everywhere. Word is they're scared. Like someone's close to their real secrets, not just rumors."

They part quietly. Natalia leaves a folded bill behind and remembers every word, every hint. She saves it all for Mariel, for Ivy, holding tight to hope that tonight might change everything—or nothing at all.

Ivy's Night Watch

Far away, in a windowless safehouse, Ivy Thompson leans over a glowing laptop. Outside, neon signs blur through cold glass, blinking faintly as dawn approaches. Phones, tangled wires, worn headphones, and empty energy drink cans surround her. Her hands move quickly, eyes tired but sharp.

Encrypted files scroll across her screen. Numbers and codes map a trail left by the Brotherhood. The path twists and turns until a payment record appears, marked with strange initials and Lucien's code—Orion—cold and calculating. Anxiety and adrenaline fill her mouth. She forces herself to breathe deeply and focus.

Her quick message to Natalia breaks the silence between distant sirens: "Nat, I have proof. Lucien's linked to the payments. If this leaks, everything changes. Making backups now. Stay safe."

Her trust in Mariel and Natalia runs deep. It grew through shared risks, late-night meetings, secret codes, and promises to shoulder the burden together. Their trust is strong, clear, but never blind.

Quiet Conversations

Natalia records a message with calm urgency. "The Brotherhood is shifting. More guards, new codes at usual places. Lucien is nervous. Meet somewhere safe."

Ivy replies shortly, "Got it. Payments?"

"Dangerous. Copy everything," Natalia answers.

"Meeting near the river, east storage, in an hour. We can't stay here."

"Copy. I'll send Mariel the drop spot."

No extra words, just the tense focus of people who know every second is precious.

Ivy's external drives blink green as backups finish. She wipes records clean while footsteps tap softly upstairs. The rhythm is uneven, maybe a threat. Her heart races. Natalia slips out the lounge's back door, keys tight in her fist, breath fogging a window as she checks behind. Danger waits, always.

They move separately but connected—each choice a risk, each breath weighed down by secrets that never should see light.

Inside Lucien Blackwell's World

City lights wrap glass buildings like electric veins in a pale morning haze. In his office, Lucien Blackwell sits behind a dark wood desk. His eyes are sharp and stormy like the skyline outside. Rain makes patterns on the windows, blurring the traffic and glowing signs. The room smells clean—vents and expensive cologne—but beneath it is the scent of ink, leather, and tension. It's a quiet threat.

His burner phone vibrates silently. The cracked screen shows a coded message from the Brotherhood. Panic hides under the data: Mariel Dawson is a problem. She carries proof of their deals. Tonight's shadows did not hide her.

He closes his eyes, seeing the network behind his world—money, fake companies, partners, judges, lobbyists—all tangled like moths around a flame. One mistake could shatter it all, spilling years of secrets. Mariel's persistence shakes the power built on suits and broken bodies, on secrets kept in boardrooms and shadowed streets. This is their kingdom, but now it teeters on the edge.

He unlocks his encrypted tablet to check records hidden behind codes. He knows how fragile everything is. One wrong move and names like Cross, Kane, and Vega will fall into the spotlight. His company, shielded by law and the Brotherhood, would crumble under subpoenas, ruined reputations, and hungry competitors.

Mariel is no easy threat to remove. He feels her close—her daring eyes from that night. Is he afraid? Or is there something colder pulling at him? Something strange about this dangerous game?

In a conference room under harsh lights, Marcus Reed stands stiff and serious. Celeste watches with folded arms. Two top enforcers wait silently. Lucien speaks clearly: erase weak links, reroute secure channels, scrub all details. Mariel Dawson's face appears on the screen—a ghost haunting them all.

"Trace everything. No mercy for loose ends. If she's a threat, we wipe the slate clean."

Celeste raises an eyebrow. "And if she isn't?"

"She will be," Lucien replies coldly. "We won't wait."

Marcus tightens his jaw. "Do you want her followed or silenced?"

Lucien taps the table slowly. "I want certainty. No surprises."

Celeste meets his gaze, old scars showing in her posture. "This game will burn people. Are you ready?"

"Who says I want anyone burned?"

"I know how this ends—bodies or betrayals. Nothing stays hidden forever."

"There's more at risk than pride."

"Then fight like it's war, not a game."

They hold their stares, heavy with memories of lost battles.

After they leave, Lucien stays silent. His face unreadable, heart tight. Below, the city glows in rain and light, uncaring who wins or loses. His thoughts roll between Mariel's brave face and the fear she brings. If she exposes them, more than the Brotherhood's power will break. His soul fights to hold on. Her courage both frightens and draws him—the conflict eats at him.

His phone buzzes again. An informant's message: rivals watch and wait, ready to strike if the Brotherhood stumbles. Names flash in his mind—Darius, Vega, Carver, Drake—each tied to his fate, each darkness closing in. A plan unfolds, bringing hunters and prey close.

He opens a hidden drawer and places a folder marked "Threats" on his desk. On top, Mariel's name, fresh ink, and her strong, defiant photo catch the light. The drawer closes with a heavy click. Lucien Blackwell faces dawn alone, war closing in from every side.

The Glass Conference Room

The glass conference room sits right in the middle of the newsroom. Its clear walls let you see everything happening inside, offering no privacy at all. Mariel holds her worn notebook and phone, both showing signs of last night's frantic efforts to find the truth. Across the black glass table, Lauren Cassidy carefully flips through a folder, sitting straight and tense like a bow ready to shoot. Outside, the city's noise fills the newsroom. Phones ring, keyboards click, editors talk in groups, and the world waits for stories it won't fully understand.

Lauren closes the folder softly but with finality. Her hazel eyes lock onto Mariel, sharp and assessing, weighing risk and loyalty at the same time. Rain streaks down the window, making the distant skyscrapers blur. Lucien Blackwell's name hangs heavily between them, still quietly discussed like a shadow casting doubt and fear.

Lauren speaks cautiously but clearly, reminding Mariel of the dangerous situation surrounding City Hall, the unions, and Blackwell's latest trial. She warns that without solid proof that can hold up in court, they can't afford to cause trouble. Mariel's pitch had named many members of the Orion Brotherhood, and Lauren asks if Mariel truly wants to take on these dangerous men. She poses hard questions: What if Mariel is wrong? What if rumors ruin her career?

Mariel's Struggle

A heavy pressure sits in Mariel's chest. Years of fighting against authority and facing loss burn within her. Memories of betrayal by mentors who turned cold and having her stories stolen fuel her determination. She catches her reflection in the glass: messy hair, a tight grip on her pen, eyes mixing hope and fear. She carries no shield, only nerve and belief.

Lauren then makes it clear how dangerous Lucien Blackwell and his group are, even more so than the crooked politicians or CEOs Mariel has reported on before. If any claim isn't solid, it could lead to lawsuits that could close down the newsroom. Lauren refuses to approve guesses or suspicions. She demands Mariel cut out anything she can't firmly prove. Facts must stand alone, or Lauren will shut the story down herself.

The voices of reporters outside cast shadows on the frosted glass, their talks seeming distant, like another world. Mariel feels the full weight of the newsroom's power behind Lauren—years of rules that say truth is only safe when backed by evidence. Lauren's calm voice carries a warning, mixed with the smell of old paper and coffee under the hum of ambition and electronics.

Standing Firm

Mariel stands up, her chair making a soft sound as she moves back. Though barely taller than Lauren, her voice is steady and firm. She says she is not trying to cause drama or risk the paper's future. She explains that every source in her notebook took big risks to talk to her. The trail points directly to Blackwell, backed by digital records, money transfers, and people willing to speak if she protects their identities.

Mariel knows the stakes but reminds Lauren she was not hired to rewrite city council press releases. If she backs down every time someone threatens her, then what is the point of journalism? The room tightens with tension, stretched like a string ready to snap. A printer starts in the distance, and someone laughs loudly in the bullpen, trying to keep things light.

Lauren's face shows frustration mixed with respect and fear. She exhales slowly, holding the folder like she's trying to crush any mistake inside it. Lauren admits she doesn't doubt Mariel's passion but warns that the city destroys idealists. The men Mariel is chasing turn lawsuits into weapons. They agree Mariel should keep digging quietly, with Lauren's support for now. But if solid evidence cannot be found, this story will become a warning example for others. Neither is untouchable.

Leaving the Room

Mariel tightens her jaw and picks up her notebook and phone, adrenaline pumping through her veins. The room feels smaller now, Lauren's shadow stretching across the table like a line not to be crossed. The news rushes on outside, relentless and unaware of the battle inside.

She doesn't look back as she opens the door and steps out. Light cuts across her face, and voices and movement pull her into the busy newsroom. The rhythm of Manhattan flows through her—pollution, energy, uncertainty—a city full of secrets daring her to uncover the truth. Every step past the desks is a quiet promise: she will not be silenced today. Yet warnings follow her closely, sharp and electric, weaving through the chaos.

Walking Through Manhattan

Manhattan's streets gleam under a light rain, the city barely slowed down by the weather. Mariel's boots splash in puddles as she moves through traffic. Cold drops hit her lips sharply. Steam rises from subway grates, wrapping around her legs and the knot in her stomach. The memory of the glass room, fogged by breath and Lauren's cold gaze, still stings inside her.

She pushes through the door of a café into warmth and quiet noise. Inside, the world softens. Small glass vases hold wildflowers on every table. Jazz plays softly beneath quiet conversations. Natalia waits at a small window table, light around her hair like a soft glow in contrast to the dark city outside. Greens like ferns and ivy create a calm space that muffles the noise of the city.

When Natalia sees Mariel, she quietly raises her hand. Mariel slides into the chair, her shoulders falling with tired relief. Her fingers tremble as she opens her notebook, still slightly damp from gripping it on the train. She skips small talk and focuses on the urgent.

Sharing the Burden

Mariel says it's always the same: Lauren thinks she wants trouble. She is told that if she doesn't have recorded confessions, then the story won't survive. She repeats how Lauren said one mistake kills the story and that she should drop the biggest story of her life. Mariel shudders, frustrated. All the late nights chasing leads feel wasted if the powerful can just bury everything. She asks if journalism is now about playing it safe.

Natalia leans in, showing understanding and careful hope. She reminds Mariel that Lauren isn't the only obstacle. Last spring, Raymond tried to kill a story about the DA for the same reasons—too risky, not enough proof, not the right time. Every newsroom has those who want applause but avoid risks.

With a quiet tap of her thumb on Mariel's hand, Natalia explains how the legal team, especially Geller, controls what gets through when panic strikes. Management cares more about fundraisers than real news. Lauren watches her phone closely for certain names for a reason.

But Natalia offers a plan. They don't have to play by these rules. They can find support from people with history, like Sato in the archives or Jana at City Records, who owe Natalia favors. Together, they can gather enough proof to make the story too big to stop.

Preparing and Planning

The clatter of a tray pulls Mariel's attention back to the café. She holds her cup, steam burning her face, the bitter smell of espresso settling, mixed with a growing sense of comfort. Natalia's voice lowers, urgent.

She promises to contact former City Hall insiders, quietly spreading the word that The Herald is digging into the Orion Club. If enough rumors start, Lauren will see that everyone is waiting for the story. Stories this big become hard to kill without drawing more attention.

Natalia squeezes Mariel's hand, promising protection. Mariel laughs and cries a little, worried that if this blows up, management will blame them both. Natalia says she'd rather fight with Mariel than watch her fall alone. They agree to keep moving together.

They fall silent in the café's soft hum. Mariel's mind swings between hope and fear, dreaming of making the headline that exposes the Brotherhood. But reality whispers that if she wins, the city will change, and powerful enemies will fight back with everything they have.

The Night's Work

Night deepens, and the city fades into dark blue through the café windows. Mariel and Natalia sit close, papers spread around them: worn notebooks, photos, receipts, and a glowing laptop. Outside, car lights streak the wet streets, and jazz plays softly, creating calm amid the tense study.

Mariel moves thoughtfully. She spreads photos: grainy shots of Lucien Blackwell getting out of an unmarked car; digital money trails Ivy decrypted, linking fake accounts to secret shell companies. Names on paper have been written and crossed out. The smell of burnt coffee and cinnamon fills the air, mixing with memories of cold alleys and whispered threats.

Natalia frowns, leaning in to study files: coded conversations, a city treasurer hinting at immunity, a former receptionist describing late deliveries to the Orion Club's back door. Silver jewelry shines in the lamp's soft glow as she points out connections between papers and screens.

Mariel opens an envelope and pulls out a business card for a defense witness, the name hastily written, phone number faded. Quietly, she comments on how well Lucien covers his tracks, making it hard to see his deep involvement even with digital evidence.

Natalia shakes her head, saying it's difficult but not impossible. Lucien moves like a ghost, and the Brotherhood's reach is wider than expected. She wonders if the receptionist, Kara, is safe to talk to. If not, they need more than digital proof or one frightened witness.

Careful Moves

Mariel agrees they cannot scare anyone. One leak, and Lucien's people will bury every name they have. Kara is scared, but her brother, an ex-marine, hates the Brotherhood. If Mariel can get Kara alone, she might speak off the record. Mariel worries most about the city treasurer—too much at stake to trust her.

Natalia plans to reach out to whistleblowers, old clients, and city clerks with grudges against the Brotherhood. She will contact them carefully, never twice by the same method. But she warns: if they slip up, the risks are huge.

Mariel's voice is sharp as lightning as she promises no mistakes. Every step will be planned: no unencrypted messages, no signs of journalism. Interviews will be face-to-face in safe spots. Mariel will conduct interviews while Natalia watches their back channels. They will keep everything off the official newsroom schedule. If asked, the story is about city redevelopment, nothing more. They will use Ivy's encrypted line only.

They organize notes carefully. Natalia stacks papers of surveillance logs, screenshots, and anonymous tips by the laptop. Mariel packs the strongest evidence—the photos, money trails, and the card linking Lucien to something far darker than a courtroom fight—into her bag.

Determined to Finish

The quiet café noise sharpens Mariel's focus. Memories flood in—her past work in dangerous places, the times police watched her closely, the betrayal when her editor exposed her source to corrupt officials. Those scars have taught her to trust only solid proof and real loyalty, like Natalia's.

Mariel sits straight, determination fierce in her eyes as night settles. She vows to finish the story no matter the cost. If anyone tries to kill it or the Brotherhood comes after them, she won't be silenced. This is her line.

Natalia nods, her hand steady on Mariel's. Streetlight shines across their papers, lighting their faces with resolve. In their small war room, every secret feels ready to be revealed. Every choice brings them closer to the storm coming over the city. As night falls on Manhattan, their fight for truth burns bright against the darkness outside.

The Silent Office Late at Night

The law offices of Blackwell & Kane were very quiet late at night. During the day, the office was full of noise—people talking, phones ringing, papers shuffling—but now, all those sounds had disappeared. Only the soft noises coming from the city outside could be heard. Far away, the traffic made a low sound, almost like a distant hum. The office had large glass windows that let in the faint glow of neon lights from the street. These lights flickered gently and cast a soft, uneasy light that bounced off the rich wooden walls inside the room. The desks, made of dark wood, were clean and shiny, reflecting the dull light. In this quiet space, the only sound was the sharp clip of Mariel's boots as she walked across the floor. She was the only person left in the office. Her footsteps were the only sign that the place was still alive. Near the exit, the last secretary watched nervously from the side. With tired eyes, she glanced between Lucien and Mariel, then quietly moved toward the elevators. She whispered a soft goodbye that quickly disappeared into the thick silence of the room.

The Meeting Gets Tense

Lucien stood behind his large desk, which was neat and organized on the surface. However, inside, he felt troubled and uneasy. The room had big windows that offered a wide view of the city. It almost felt as if he could reach out and touch the buildings below by leaning forward. Lucien motioned toward a chair in front of his desk, inviting Mariel to sit. But she did not accept the offer and shook her head. Closing the door firmly behind her, Mariel stood straight with her arms crossed, presenting a strong image as if daring Lucien to break the silence or show any weakness. The air between them was filled with tension, heavy and almost physical.

After a moment, Lucien spoke clearly and sharply. He told Mariel that her latest article was libelous. Libel is when someone writes false statements about another person or group that can harm their reputation. Lucien accused Mariel's article of containing false claims linked to his law firm, saying it could damage how people perceived them. He said she was trying to connect his firm to a criminal scheme based on evidence he called weak and unreliable. Lucien warned that her work could bring serious legal trouble not only to his firm but could also ruin her career and the newspaper for which she wrote. His voice remained calm, but underneath, there was a hidden threat in his words.

Mariel's Strong Answer

Mariel looked at Lucien without fear. She held his gaze directly, her chin held high. The orange light from the city outside illuminated her face, making her appear clear and strong. Her expression silently challenged Lucien. She asked if his words were just empty threats or if the legal fight they both expected was about to begin. Mariel accused Lucien of defending men involved in large money laundering crimes.

Money laundering is the process by which people try to hide the origin of illegally obtained money, making it appear legal. She spoke about the Orion Brotherhood—a secret criminal group said to have influence everywhere. Mariel claimed their power reached far, even if Blackwell & Kane was not officially connected on paper. She spoke with steady confidence, demonstrating that she truly believed what she stated.

Lucien did not step back or change his stance. Inside, his mind raced to process everything Mariel said. The tense atmosphere in the room grew heavier, like the quiet just before a storm breaks. He insisted that just because someone says something does not mean it is true. He called Mariel's claims reckless and careless. Lucien promised that if she continued publishing stories about the Brotherhood, his firm would fight back using the law. This could include legal orders to stop the stories before they were printed, lawsuits claiming her words were false and hurtful, and anything else the law allowed.

Presenting the Proof

Mariel answered clearly and confidently. She said she had proof to back up her story. This proof included wire transfers, which are electronic payments sent between different banks showing suspicious money movements. She also had witness statements—reports from people who saw or knew about illegal activities. She insisted that her evidence was strong and could not be easily ignored. Despite this, she questioned Lucien's beliefs. Out loud, she wondered when he stopped caring about right and wrong and started only caring about protecting his law firm. This indicated that their conflict was more than just facts. It was a fight about morals, values, and what each person believed in.

Lucien's calm suddenly wavered. He remembered past cases that weighed on his mind. One night, a man named Markus Reed was found injured in a stairwell after a deal with the Brotherhood failed.

Lucien also recalled a past arbitration—a type of confidential legal meeting—that nearly exposed a hidden criminal operation because of a small mistake. These memories illustrated the burden Lucien carried. He had a duty to keep dangerous secrets safe and was accustomed to managing difficult problems. But this time felt different. Mariel's words struck too close to the truth and threatened to break the careful balance he had maintained.

A Quiet Warning

Leaning forward, Lucien lowered his voice. He issued a quiet warning that some truths were better left hidden. He hinted that there were very powerful groups in the city, groups stronger than ordinary criminals or corrupt politicians. His words suggested real dangers and revealed the side of him that had seen too much. This moment exposed cracks in Lucien's tough image—a man caught between following the law and protecting darker secrets. Outside, the city moved on, its life full of hidden battles and dangers invisible to most people.

Mariel's Firm Position

Mariel watched Lucien closely. She didn't see a famous lawyer or a great thinker, but a person hiding behind a tough mask. She felt some anger inside, but also a small sympathy she did not want to admit. She told Lucien she was not easily scared and would not be controlled by hidden warnings or threats. She stated that if the Brotherhood was innocent, then Lucien had nothing to worry about from her articles. But if her evidence was true, she promised to continue pursuing the story, no matter what. Mariel also vowed to protect her sources—the people who helped her gather information—and would never reveal their identities. Her determination was clear and strong.

The Meeting Comes to an End

Lucien wished he could feel the same confidence he once had when he believed everything could be controlled by contracts and fear. Now, things felt unstable. Mariel's strong drive and belief in justice were real, unlike the false fronts Lucien was accustomed to. For a moment, he wondered what it would be like to have that faith too.

Mariel stood tall, refusing Lucien's last attempts to ease the tension. Her face was calm but steady, her determination like a quiet but powerful storm. Lucien stood up and motioned toward the door, trying to remain calm, though his hands gripped the desk tightly. Mariel did not rush. She walked slowly and carefully. As she passed by him, her determination felt like a sudden shock in the quiet office.

After she left, the office air smelled of coffee and leather, mixed with a heavy feeling that lingered. Alone, Lucien let his calm facade fall, revealing his worry. He understood this problem was bigger than any he had faced before. Outside, the city lit up with bright lights and hidden secrets, alive and watching, waiting to see what would happen next.

Dangerous Desires

The lounge feels broken, made up of shadows and the quiet stress of money. The gold wall lights shine through blue glass, casting a dim glow that makes the velvet and wood look stuck in a fake twilight. Lucien enters through a side door, his reflection bending and hard to recognize in the gold door frame. Outside, the city is loud and busy, but inside the smoked windows, thick carpets and the smell of old tobacco keep the noise low. Lucien moves quickly and confidently. The staff seem to know the rules and move aside for him without being told. With one look, he asks for a private room and says quietly but firmly, "No interruptions, no matter who asks."

He sits in the darkest booth, where the corners seem to close in, holding secrets in the shadows. The table smells faintly of lemon oil mixed with spilled whiskey—clean in one way, messy in another. He rolls a crystal glass between his thumb and finger. The soft sound is small but sharp, like a warning before something serious happens. He watches the door carefully, ready for danger or an offer. Inside, memories press on him: his law office, now quiet and empty, the sting of Mariel's accusations still fresh. He tells himself this meeting is just a way to control things. But deep down, he feels nervous in a way he can't explain.

Mariel enters the lounge, framed by neon light from outside. She stops, each move full of purpose. Her shoulders are stiff, and her eyes shift between the bar and dark corners where powerful people quietly make deals and betray one another. She looks for escape routes, then sees Lucien and studies him closely for signs of threat. She walks over, her heels clicking softly but sending a message to those paying attention.

She sits close to Lucien, the space between them full of tension. Light falls on his sharp features and eyes like dark glass. Mariel refuses to hide anything; her purse sits on the table like a shield, and her dark hair falls across her jaw as she meets his gaze directly.

"You care too much about my cases for just watching," Lucien says softly but sharply. His voice is like a sharp blade wrapped in soft cloth. "Tell me you're not trying to hurt more people with your stories. Or are you after my reputation?"

Mariel thinks about the story she's chasing—following leads through back alleys and late-night emails, uncovering lives ruined by the Orion Brotherhood's reach. Her voice matches his control, but there's suspicion in her words. "I want the truth," she says. "I don't choose which names get burned, Lucien. But for someone so careful, you're at the center of every crime I track. That can't be luck."

Their words clash, with something unspoken between them. Mariel's fingers brush her phone, ready to run or reveal secrets. Lucien watches her, noticing small signs—the twitch of her mouth, the tension in her shoulders. He senses the question she won't ask, a silent challenge to trust her if he can. Inside, old habits fight new feelings.

He is torn between being the fixer who solves everything and the man who can't fix his own broken heart.

He lets silence hang, then slowly sips whiskey. The burn grounds him, holding back what he wants to admit. He leans in slightly and says softly, under the lounge's music hum, "You think you know this world, but the rot isn't just on the surface, Mariel. It's everywhere. You can't expose the monster without feeding it." His voice holds tiredness, something only she might notice—a fragile feeling under his defense.

For a moment, Mariel's face softens—not with trust but with the exhaustion of chasing shadows. She reaches for her phone, and her hand touches Lucien's on the table. The touch feels electric—her skin warm, his cold as stone. The world seems to shrink, the background noise fading into this moment.

Lucien doesn't move. He laces his fingers with hers, holding her hand between them. His face stays calm, but his eyes show the weight of what's happening—a silent plea for something neither can name.

Their breathing slows and falls together. The city's noise fades into something personal and risky. Their hands stay linked, Lucien steady but weighing danger and mercy. He wonders if this fragile peace will last or if it's a trap they're both making tighter with every secret left unsaid. Outside, the city goes on, unaware, while two opposites hover between surrender and fight, neither willing to break the spell.

Lucien leads Mariel to a private room. The silence is deep, deeper than any place in the city's secret corners. Thick velvet curtains block the outside world, muffling even distant horns and sirens from Manhattan's late night. A faint city light slips from the curtains' edges, shining on crystal glasses left on a shiny sideboard. When Lucien closes the door, the click sounds louder than usual, like a quiet promise in the small, secret room.

Lucien's usual calm fades when he faces Mariel. She stands by a window where neon light faintly reflects on the glass. Her shape is outlined in cold blue. The air between them feels thick and smoky. He straightens but then relaxes a bit. A softness shows in his jaw, and his hand hangs uncertainly at his side.

"I thought I wasn't afraid," he says quietly, losing the confidence he often shows in court. "But I'm not. Not with you here. Not with everything about to fall apart." His words are soft, revealing something he rarely shows. Maybe regret or hope; even he isn't sure.

He watches her carefully. Mariel stands with her back to the window, arms crossed as if holding herself together. "All this digging, every lead and name, has left me alone," she says, her voice raw. "No one trusts someone who asks too many questions. I can't remember the last time I felt safe." She stumbles on the last word, as if admitting the truth hurts.

The air trembles between them. Lucien moves closer, closing the space step by step. His hand lifts but stops before touching her face, as if asking permission. When his thumb gently brushes her jaw, she leans into it, lowering her guard a little. For a moment, Lucien sees beyond suspicion, catching a glimpse of the girl she might have been before fear and betrayal hardened her voice.

He lowers his head, and their lips meet. What starts gentle quickly becomes fierce, full of longing and the fragile peace they share. Every touch warns: danger is close. Mariel's hands grip his shirt like an anchor, and Lucien tightens his hold with urgency—a man wanting what he can't control. Desire breaks through their control. If the world outside exploded, they wouldn't hear it.

Afterward, silence fills the room, broken only by their breathing and the distant hum of traffic. Lucien's heart pounds in a way he rarely feels—loud and fast. Vulnerability mocks him, showing what he tries to hide: in Mariel's arms, he is not untouchable.

Their fingers stay tangled, unwilling to let go. Mariel's eyes scan him, full of wariness and hope, as if looking for a catch in their quiet room. She whispers, her voice shaking, "You hide so much. I don't know which part is the real you."

His voice roughens. "I owe debts I can't pay. Lines I won't cross—except to protect what's left of me." His words sound like a raw confession from deep inside.

"You're still hiding," she says, her voice trembling. "Maybe I am too. Maybe we don't know how to be honest anymore."

Lucien gently rubs her knuckles with his thumb. Trust here is sharp—both a risk and a gift, heavy like the city outside. He looks deep into her eyes, wanting to know if she's honest or hiding something else. Mariel meets his gaze, listening for lies or past betrayals she knows well. In this quiet closeness, doubt and desire mix, every breath full of unspoken things.

Control slips from Lucien the longer he stays; his heart bruised by hunger and suspicion. The Brotherhood's rules and his careful plans seem meaningless compared to what it costs to let Mariel reach him, body and soul. That scares him more than any danger.

They finally sit side by side, the city breathing softly beyond the curtains. Their skin still warm from closeness, but cold space slowly grows. Between their slow heartbeats and silence, caught in light sheets and heavy thoughts, Lucien feels the cost of giving in: parts of himself he can't lose, secrets he won't share, and the longing that hums even here where they are most vulnerable. The line between partner and enemy, lover and rival, stays blurry and weak as dawn's first light touches the window.

Mariel stands before a gold-framed mirror, pulling at the cuffs of her blouse. Her dark hair falls softly around her ears, and faint marks from Lucien's touch are hidden beneath her collar. The room feels heavy and quiet, like smoke, while distant sounds of Manhattan drift in through dark windows—the hiss of tires on wet streets, the far wail of sirens. These sounds remind her that comfort and chaos mix on nights like this.

Her phone rests on a narrow marble shelf, the screen dark but filled with unsent messages. Mariel looks at herself in the mirror: lips tight, eyes red from sleepless nights. There is a fire inside her chest, a pain made of guilt and desire. This battle is not new, but never in such a dangerous place. Regret flares sharply when she thinks of Lucien's mouth on hers, the promises whispered in sighs, the vows she thought she'd never make. She wonders if the mirror might crack under all the uncertainty and secret longings she carries.

Memories of past betrayals swirl in her mind; old wounds sting beneath new skin. Every instinct says to be careful, but that caution weakens after sharing so many secrets. Her thumb hovers over the phone's unlock button, as if this small move might shift things toward truth or disaster. The faint smell of Lucien's cologne—pepper, cold, and danger—hangs in the air. In this quiet moment, regret and reckless desire circle, pushing her to find a way forward without breaking completely.

A shadow falls across her shoulder. Lucien stands in the doorway, relaxed but powerful. "You should be careful," he says softly, his usual control hiding worry.

"I know how to take care of myself," Mariel answers sharply, the rawness gone from her voice. "This isn't my first tough story, Lucien."

He watches her, unreadable, jaw tight from an earlier bruise. "Not every story ends the way you want."

Mariel's breath catches. Words hang unspoken, filled with suspicion, longing, and pride. Lucien looks at her hands, as if testing if she'll run or break. His concern hides behind a mask, but it's clear.

She walks past him, her coat brushing his fingers softly but barely noticed. Her steps are quick and sure; she holds her head high and doesn't look back. The heavy silence swallows the sound of her retreat, the red carpet softening her footsteps until the suite door slides shut behind her. Lucien stands in half-light, hand on his jaw where old scars tighten with memory. His figure blurs—part man, part threat—caught between roles he knows too well.

His phone suddenly buzzes, breaking the silence. The screen glows cold with an unknown number and one message: She's not alone—watch your back. His pulse tightens. The warning spins through his mind like a blade in a dark room. He pictures faces from the Brotherhood—Caius, Darius, Orion, Silas—any one of them could be behind this threat. Or maybe Damien, brooding in dark corners; Elias, with secrets even Lucien cannot read; or someone closer—a quiet voice meant to destroy trust.

Down the hall, Mariel's phone vibrates. The name Ivy glows in blue. She hesitates, then answers.

"Someone's leaking, Mariel," Ivy says, voice tight and urgent. "This isn't a rumor. Cassidy wants you to back off—she thinks there's a mole in the newsroom. Someone's giving them info, maybe watching you. Please promise me, don't trust anyone tonight. Not even me."

Suspicion grows in Mariel's eyes. Ivy, usually steady but restless, now seems another risky piece. Cassidy, pushing deadlines but protective, might be hiding something or trying to keep the office safe. Even Natalia, usually steady, might be scared or ambitious. Every alliance feels fragile; every secret is dangerous.

If Lucien's world is full of locked doors and secret codes, Mariel's is a forest of threats she can't see. Every whisper or call might be the knife that cuts her out. She wonders how many nights will pass before even Lucien's rough kindness becomes a danger. If he suffers for her, who else will get hurt? And if she pulls away, hides behind armor that kept her safe since the first betrayal, will anything be left for them except ashes and regret?

Mariel stands on the dark stairwell leading outside, phone trembling in hand. Lucien is above, standing quietly, eyes fixed on the mirror, his own phone full of danger. The city's heartbeat pulses in the walls, but inside, trust shrinks—a quiet space that links them, a fragile peace held by the weight of betrayal waiting outside every door.

The Rainy City and the Industrial Wasteland

Rain seeps into every crack of the city late at night, turning broken asphalt into streaks of silver. Mariel leads the way through the industrial area, a bleak stretch of concrete and steel that makes Manhattan feel distant and unfamiliar. Old warehouses stand silent, their walls covered in graffiti that barely shows under the faint light of a single, flickering streetlamp. The quiet of the night is only broken by the sound of heavy breaths and the crunch of stones beneath three pairs of boots. The air carries the smell of grease, crumbling bricks, and cold metal, all waiting just before the storm hits.

Mariel's hands tremble, but not from fear. She wouldn't admit it even to herself. The tension inside her rises with every step she takes into danger, knowing there's no sure promise of returning home safely. In her hand is a crumpled piece of paper with a rough number code, written by a gloved hand just hours before. When she finally finds the warehouse's rusty side door, covered in faded warnings and peeling paint, she lets out a breath, punches the code into the worn keypad, and waits. For a moment, the rain is the only sound. Then a loud metal click echoes, and the door creaks open, swallowing them one by one ins ide.

Inside the Warehouse

The air inside is still and stale, their breath hanging in front of them in clouds. The smell is sharp—old oil, mold, and chemicals that cling like sweat to the walls and floors. Mariel switches on her flashlight, sending a beam cutting through the darkness. The light lands on piles of crates stacked against concrete walls. Some crates are made of broken wood with stamped numbers, while others hide black metal parts sticking out. Guns—more guns than she's ever seen, except in her worst nightmares or the darkest stories she's covered. Some guns have no markings, untraceable and deadly, waiting in the shadows.

Natalia moves quietly, crouching near shelves, holding a camera that clicks and whirs softly as she takes pictures. She pushes aside a box spilling greasy stacks of hundred-dollar bills. There are no bands or bank logos, just a messy pile of money. Loose papers fall out, some stamped clearly, others filled with coded writing that Mariel's gut recognizes immediately as Brotherhood messages. Nearby, Ivy moves toward old worktables, checking power strips and scanning blueprints taped to the walls. She finds three dusty plastic USB drives taped under one of the tables.

Mariel knows this is where real power hides. The city's decay is not just physical but a sign of control. The Brotherhood's influence spreads deep into every poisoned part of this forgotten place. No one watches here except them. There's no law except the rules enforced by money and violence, carried out by men nobody ever sees. The real power beats quietly beneath Manhattan's skin, not in fancy office towers, but in this half-ruined, ignored wasteland.

Danger Strikes

Suddenly, Ivy's calm voice breaks, trembling slightly. "Hey—look up." Above them, a long crack rolls across a concrete beam, too wide to be ignored. Before Mariel can warn anyone, the floor shudders beneath their feet. A sharp, dangerous metal sound follows. Natalia looks up just in time as the ceiling breaks apart and plaster starts falling in thin, choking strips.

"Move!" Natalia shouts, panic ringing in her voice. Dust swirls thick around them, gritty on their tongues as plaster hits the ground like rain. The warehouse groans loudly, metal screaming over their pounding footsteps as they run for safety.

Mariel shouts directions, "Tunnel—left!" She clutches the worn folder stolen from a crate—the prize that makes all the risk worth it. Ivy gasps for breath, Natalia curses loudly, and they sprint past falling debris and screeching, twisting steel bars. The terrible sound of collapsing brick and metal fills the air behind them, a dangerous chase.

Outside and Safe, But Tense

Once they burst into the narrow alley, rain stings their faces, mixing with sweat and dust. Mariel slides down against a cold brick wall covered in graffiti. Her muscles scream with exhaustion, and her lungs burn from the cold air. She pulls out the soggy folder from her bag, hands shaking. The folder holds coded pages, secret contracts signed with just initials, and addresses she half remembers from tips and warnings.

Natalia sits nearby, clutching her camera, the lens smudged with dust, her breathing shallow. Ivy wipes grit from her neck, her chest rising and falling quickly. Above them, the warehouse wall collapses one last time with a thunderous crash that briefly drowns out the rain.

The rain feels colder now. The three women huddle close, backs pressed against the brick, quietly holding what they've taken from the city's hidden empire. High above, city lights glow—clean and distant, unaware of the danger below. In the shadows of the ruins, three women breathe hard, their nerves raw, a mixture of fear and hope filling the cold night air.

Tensions Rise at Mariel's Apartment

Later, Natalia drops her bag heavily onto the gray sofa, breaking a heavy silence in Mariel's apartment. Rain streaks down the window in jagged lines, casting broken light across gray walls and teal pillows. The room usually feels warmer after nights like this—small and crowded, everything smelling stronger, exhaustion present in the air. But tonight, it doesn't feel that way. Natalia breathes shallowly, hands trembling as she pulls a worn bag strap from her shoulder, her eyes dark with worry.

"You got in too fast," Natalia says sharply. "How, Ivy? The code resets every seventy-two hours, and we just changed it yesterday." There's fear and suspicion in her voice. Ivy avoids eye contact, her thumbs scrolling nervously on her phone, headphones hanging loose around her neck. The glow of the phone screen highlights her uneasy eyes.

"It's not a big deal," Ivy replies in a short, harsh voice. "I just reset the security. We had to get inside."

Natalia folds her arms, her lip trembling. "You didn't hesitate. Most people would need minutes. You didn't even blink. Who else could get into that system? You sent a text when we walked in, didn't you?"

"I was just checking the signal," Ivy answers, frowning as she slips her phone into her hoodie pocket.

"Right. Sure," Natalia's voice cracks with doubt.

The room fills with tension, despite the soft pillows and stacks of notebooks around them. The cat is missing. Mariel stands quietly between the two, feeling the air crackle with mistrust. She tastes old coffee on her tongue and cold rain in her breath.

"Natalia, Ivy. Enough." Mariel's voice is calm but firm. Both women glare at her. "We have bigger threats than each other. Fighting now is exactly what the Brotherhood wants." She puts a hand on Natalia's shoulder, feeling the tightness there, then looks at Ivy, who keeps glancing nervously at the door.

"We have to be honest," Mariel says quietly, "If anyone has doubts, now's the time to speak. We need each other, or none of this works." Her words are more a plea than a command.

Natalia's face softens slightly, like the calm in a storm's eye. Ivy drops her shoulders, her jaw clenched as if holding back pain.

Suddenly, Ivy stands and moves to a cluttered desk. "I got a ping," she says, fingers tapping fast on the old wood. "During the break-in—I found a wireless signal sniffing my device. It wasn't just city noise. Someone was watching us. Maybe following us for a while."

Natalia pales, folding her arms even tighter. "You could be in danger. So could Mariel's bag. Anything we took might be leaking. Anyone could be listening now. How long did you know?"

"I found it right after we left the warehouse. I've been wiping logs as fast as I can," Ivy answers quickly, defensive. "I'm fine, Nat. But whoever's watching... they're good."

Mariel feels a cold fear running through her skin. She moves to the window, opening it slightly. Rain hits her face as she looks down at the empty, shiny street. City lights scatter across the wet pavement. She's tired, but adrenaline is keeping her awake. Her mind spins with faces in shadows, lost or hidden signals, and threats lurking in digital messages.

Trust feels fragile, nearly a joke. Paranoia runs through her veins. She looks at Natalia's hunched shoulders and Ivy's avoiding eyes. Her heart pounds. If betrayal comes, it will be quiet, close, and personal.

She remembers the Brotherhood's reach, breaking into safe places and alliances, breaking trust until only doubt remains. It's not just crumbling buildings that are dangerous but also the fragile network of loyalty she's held onto. She recalls laughter in this small apartment, warmth pushing against the city's chill. Tonight, mistrust makes the room colder than the rain outside.

She decides to meet less often, to encrypt every message, to stop trusting screens. They will meet face to face only and share secrets quietly, eyes locked, breath visible in the cold air.

Natalia grips her knees on the edge of the sofa. Her eyes look empty in the dim light. Ivy sits beside her, hiding in her hoodie, fingers wrapped around her own knee, barely breathing. The city's glowing lights shift colors over rain-soaked glass. No one speaks. Nothing soothes their nerves or the loneliness between them.

The three women are close but tense, each weighing risks and secrets, counting the cost of letting their guard down. Outside, distant sirens remind them that nothing is safe—not here, not now.

Danger Returns on the Empty Street

The night air outside is sharp and wet, hanging quietly over empty streets. Mariel steps out of her building, clutching the stolen folder to her chest, stepping carefully on broken, wet pavement. A flickering streetlamp casts long shadows on the sidewalk. For a moment, she thinks no one is watching.

Leather shoes scrape the pavement. Glass crunches under heavy footsteps. Two figures emerge from a dark alley, faces hidden, long coats drifting loosely. They block Mariel's path. She lowers her chin, clutching the folder tight, the cold biting her wrists. Then a third figure moves silently from the shadows—a man.

Lucien moves quickly, like a man dodging fate. His body twists—a shoulder moves, an elbow sweeps, arms fight with skill learned on streets and courts. The first attacker falls with a broken bone's snap and surprise. The second swings, but Lucien twists away, his jacket flaring as he grabs the man's wrist and pins him to the wet wall.

For a moment, only Mariel's heavy breathing fills the air. Lucien stares coldly at the stunned attacker, then lets him drop next to his friend, both unconscious. The city noise rushes back: a motorcycle roaring, rain hitting gutters, panic surging in Mariel's chest.

Lucien grabs Mariel's elbow, firm but not harsh. He leads her into a narrow space hidden from the streetlamp's glow. Brick walls press cold against their backs. His voice is low and steady. "Tonight was a warning. They know you have something the Brotherhood can't lose."

She looks up, chin steady. "That was more than a warning. I saw it in their eyes."

"Rogue hands, not Brotherhood enforcers," Lucien says, jaw tight, a faint scar marking his face in the dark. "Some think chaos is a tool. They forget chaos burns everything."

Rain slides down Mariel's sleeve as she holds the folder tight. "You mean it will get worse."

Lucien pauses. The danger hangs heavy between them. He should turn away, tell her to disappear, let this end now. But instead, he watches raindrops in her hair, hears the rawness in her voice. In another life, he might tell her the truth without anything but hope.

But he pushes the feeling down. He belongs to the Brotherhood—with its lies, debts, and secret wars. Protecting her would mean betraying everything else. Still, in the half-dark, he wants what he cannot have—a life for her without fear, a man she can trust in daylight.

Lucien leans in, raindrops falling from his shoulders. "You made it through tonight, but the city is hunting you. Not just my enemies, but others who want to kill the Brotherhood—and anyone who takes from it. You're not safe."

Mariel meets his eyes, steady and strong. "I never was. I can't walk away, even if you ask me."

He almost smiles, remembering the sound of her laughter once—ordinary, bright. He wants to ask her to stop, just for tonight, to step back from danger and let him finish this where it belongs. But the city is already changing: power shifting, alliances breaking. The chain tying him to the Brotherhood and her to the truth is the same.

Guilt chokes him, but she would never forgive his secrets. Behind his mask of fighter and protector, something breaks. Tonight, he is something more: a desperate builder of impossible futures. Failure will cost them both.

"Every step, every message—someone watches. Trust no one you can't see," Lucien warns, his voice rough and soft, coming from deep inside.

"Then I'll leave the light on," Mariel says with a weak, brave smile. "But I won't run. You know that."

He lets go of her arm, brushing rain from his sleeve, a tired smile touching his lips.

"You never do."

For a moment, neither moves—two survivors in a city where secrets taste like smoke. Neon lights blur on wet streets, sirens wail through the rain. Their shadows blend on the ground, neither ready to fade.

Mariel steps from the corner. Her courage shines faintly. Lucien watches her disappear into the night, a quiet ache pressing deep. Above them, unseen players in the city move, planning the next step.

Fractures Within

The damp smell of concrete and cold machines clings to Marcus Reed's skin as he steps into the Brotherhood's hideout—if you can call a windowless, box-like room with buzzing fluorescent lights and the scent of old blood in the grout a hideout. The heavy steel door slams shut behind him. Six faces appear and disappear in the shadows, sitting around a worn table covered with security reports and crushed cigarette packs. The papers curl from the humidity. Trust has shrunk away, pulled back from the group.

Marcus's boots scrape against the rough floor. He looks around: Ivan Petrov leans back with his arms crossed, a tight smile on his broad face; Alicia Rivera's sharp, dark eyes meet his, her hands still on a folder marked URGENT. The others, both experienced and young hotheads, stiffen as Marcus stands tall. His jaw tightens, muscles drawn tight with the memory of the recent attack, the price paid in lost men and ruined secrets.

He slams his hand on the steel table, the sound echoing through the safe house. "How," Marcus says, his voice hard as glass, "did this happen? Who missed it?"

Ivan sneers. "Don't blame me, Reed. I followed orders—it wasn't my job to watch the safehouse tech."

Alicia cuts in sharply. "Maybe if people didn't hand out access codes so freely, we wouldn't be exposed like this."

"You saying that's my fault?" Ivan pushes back, his chair screeching. "You're the one who left the back channel open. Did your friends at the Herald warn you, Alicia?"

Voices flare like fire in dry grass—shouting about surveillance mistakes and loyalty; another mutters about the long shadow of Lucien Blackwell, stirring old anger and fear. Marcus listens, the noise scraping on his nerves.

"They're killing us from the inside," he growls at Ivan. "You left that safehouse unlocked. You let them find our escape routes. What did you expect?"

Ivan bares his teeth. "You think you're better, Reed? Maybe if you spent less time following Kane and more time on the streets—"

Alicia rocks in her chair. "You can't see we're on the edge. One more mistake and Manhattan will eat us alive. But you just point fingers."

Marcus's vision narrows, adrenaline rushing through him. His first thought is to lash out and take control before the Brotherhood breaks apart. But his voice holds steady, filled with the memories of lost brothers, betrayals, and blood that will never wash away.

He looks from face to face. Ivan's sneer. Alicia's hard eyes. The restless bodies, the fear in the air, old grudges, and debts. What they have isn't true trust. It is a bond made by need. Each person hides wounds and keeps score. Tonight, the cracks grow bigger.

"What's the use," Marcus spits, "of blind loyalty that sends us to die? How many more will we bury before Kane changes? Or do we keep walking off the cliff just because we're ordered?"

Ivan explodes, pointing at Marcus. "You're the traitor! You're the only one saying this."

Others tense, caught between pride and fear. The air feels ready to snap.

"Watch it," Marcus says, cold as ice, "or you'll end up like the last fool who challenged me."

Silence falls. Heat gathers in every corner. Someone breathes sharply. Another's knuckles turn white on a coffee mug.

Marcus stares down Ivan, but there's no winning here. The wounds are too deep. He's supposed to hold these people together. For what? So Kane can run them through more disasters, fooling himself he's in control while the walls close in? Old loyalties shake Marcus's resolve—ten years of fights and smoke-filled rooms, brotherhood written in scars. But his faith breaks, bit by bit.

"I'm asking if Kane can lead," Marcus says quietly, sharp as broken glass. "How many more will die before someone says enough?"

The room falls into awkward silence. Alicia looks away, worn down; years of cleaning up after men like Kane and Ivan weigh on her. Ivan mutters "coward," but it barely breaks the quiet.

Marcus turns and storms out. Behind him, chairs scrape, and the group breaks into uneasy alliances—only wary looks remain, old scores surfacing as new doubts. The heavy door swings open, the cold city air cutting through the heat of the fight. He hesitates, feeling isolated and uneasy. He looks back. The Brotherhood is breaking more with every beat. Inside, only silence remains, except for the shallow breaths of six dangerous strangers who no longer trust each other as brothers.

Lucien Blackwell stands in his office, city lights shining silently through the tall windows. Headlines and crime laws reflect faintly on the walls, a symbol of power now under quiet attack. His phone vibrates again. Encrypted messages appear: Marcus Reed. Brotherhood safehouse. Outburst. Problem. Division. The words cut sharper than the cold rain hitting the glass—the Brotherhood's calm surface cracking under hidden storms.

He listens to voice messages filled with panic and blame. The familiar voices of men he has trusted now speak with suspicion. They mention Marcus, traitors, carelessness, and secrets lost. Lucien's jaw tightens as Marcus's angry voice plays over and over. The safehouse, once silent, is now filled with anger.

He taps the heavy glass table, then calls his three lieutenants: Lorenzo Mendez, sharp and tough; Sasha Valenko, quick but angry from past mistakes; and Victor Tran, calm and unreadable. The meeting isn't optional. They arrive in the conference room smelling of leather, ozone, and cold coffee. Outside, Manhattan's towers blink like secret signals, endless and hidden.

Lucien stays silent. City lights wash over the table scattered with blueprints, breach reports, and surveillance info—organized chaos. He looks each officer in the eye—measured, studying.

"Let's find out exactly how our house caught fire," he says coldly. "Marcus's outburst is just a sign, not the cause. I want to know who left the door open."

Victor speaks softly. "Ivan managed the safehouse schedule. He passed off his duties too quickly. I tried to cover, but—"

"No excuses," Lucien cuts in. "If our patterns are known, someone inside gave them away. Not a mistake. A choice." He flips a paper, the sound harsh. "Sasha, twelve hours ago you changed the security feeds. Why?"

She tenses, her eyes flicking to her teammates. "It was for Marcus's new protocol—he asked—" Her voice trails off in the silence.

Lucien's gaze sharpens. "When you reroute without checking, you create blind spots. Consider this a warning: loyalty is rewarded here—betrayal is punished. Understand?"

Sasha nods slightly, stiff. Lorenzo studies Sasha and then Victor, weighing loyalties.

"Temper's too high for Ivan to lead now," Lucien says with steel in his voice. "Victor, you will handle all staff checks for now. Anyone disagree?"

"One more change in leadership," Lorenzo says dryly, "and you'll face more than sharp words, Lucien."

"I prefer mutiny over sabotage," Lucien replies. "But anyone fanning these flames answers to me. Or Kane. And Kane's patience is famous—until it ends."

The room turns cold. Four figures framed by city lights, each hiding thoughts. Lucien's eyes catch Victor's calm, Sasha's masked doubt, Lorenzo's sharp mind. The Brotherhood is built on deals like this, but now the ground shakes and cracks spread under every claim of control.

Lorenzo is the first to stand, his chair scraping softly. "You want unity. Win for us. Or at least stop the bleeding." He pauses, a quiet warning that fear won't hold all loyalty. One by one, the room empties. Sasha gazes at Lucien with regret or warning as the door closes behind them.

Alone, Lucien returns to silence. The city's pulse glows outside—amber lights shining through rain and smoke. He watches his own reflection—sharp suit hiding a worn man inside. Victory always meant control. Now it tastes bitter, like rust.

In his mind, futures unfold, each worse than the last. One where Marcus's anger spreads, turning hearts hungry for a clear path. Where Sasha, pushed too hard, betrays or exposes the group to the police, ruining years of secret work. Or worse—where Elias Kane takes over with brutal force, destroying friends and enemies alike. Lucien can't see which danger will strike first—the Brotherhood falling apart inside or enemies outside getting closer.

He thinks of Mariel, her memory cutting through the noise—smart, tough, honest in a dangerous way. The lines between enemy and ally, justice and survival blur. Does he want forgiveness, or just another day on a crumbling throne? If she finds out too much, will he protect the Brotherhood or destroy it?

All empires break. He knows this, watching a drop of rain fall alone on the glass. Tonight the Brotherhood is his, but every choice pulls the noose tighter. He stares at his reflection—a man of law and crime, balanced on a sharp edge, unsure what judgment waits when the city wakes.

Lucien stands at the window, the city spread below, jaw set with the heavy task of holding a kingdom that trembles under his hands.

The café smells strongly of burnt coffee and cinnamon, thick enough to hide the city's noise outside the steamy windows. In a dark back booth, Mariel Dawson watches the nervous shaking of Jamie Lee's fingers as he slides a folded paper across the table. His eyes glance nervously to the door—fear like he's hiding from danger that might fall at any moment.

Mariel lets the old paper rest between her hand and notebook, feeling the tension from Jamie. He's sweating not from heat, but from secrets. She leans close, speaking low over the café sounds, her voice soft but firm.

"Jamie, I need to know exactly what was said at that meeting. Were they just arguing, or is someone really planning to break away?"

Jamie swallows hard, staring at a chipped mug. "You don't understand, Mariel. Since the breach, everyone's fighting. Marcus accused Ivan, blamed Alicia—it was chaos. But information is leaking. I heard people say Marcus won't take orders anymore, and some want to follow him, while others want him gone. It's more than rumors now."

Mariel breathes in the mix of smells—bitter coffee, stale fruit, sweat from a long shift—grounding herself as she asks more.

"And Kane? Are they trying to remove him, or just question his choices?"

Jamie nervously tears a napkin into strips. "Some say Kane's losing it. Too many mistakes, too many dead. Marcus won't say it straight, but I think he knows the Brotherhood's lost direction." He looks up, eyes wide. "Please, Mariel. If they find out I spoke..."

"If this leaks, I won't say your name. But tell me—has Marcus mentioned going to the police or working with outsiders?"

Jamie turns pale. "Not yet. But after tonight, I'm not sure. He just walked out. Didn't look back."

Mariel closes her notebook softly. "You did the right thing. You know how to reach me if anything else happens."

Jamie jumps up, almost tipping his chair, then disappears into the crowd of late afternoon customers. Mariel watches steam curl through the dusty light, her heart pounding in the quiet that follows.

She orders another bitter coffee to stay sharp and opens her laptop, fingers moving over encrypted files. Jamie's note lists names: Ivan, Alicia, Marcus, and others tied to accusations and betrayals. Mariel matches them with digital clues from past weeks—strange burner phone calls near the club, odd ATM cashouts after meetings, snippets of police talk Ivy decoded at night. She weaves together Jamie's fear and these clues, feeling tension knot in her stomach.

Outside, the day fades. Mariel moves through the crowd, her reflection stretching in rain-streaked windows. Down the street, two men in dark jackets talk in low voices—snatches of Russian and English.

"Think Marcus will hold? He's reckless—he'll bring us down."

"Doesn't matter. Ivan's tired of his show. Kane won't last much longer if you ask me."

Mariel quietly raises her phone, hidden by her coat sleeve. The camera clicks silently as she takes their photo—the worn car at the curb, part of a license plate shining in the fading light. Her heart races, feeling the risk of moving closer to danger.

Thoughts twist and snap as she stands under an awning, notebook tight against her chest. Jamie's pale face joins the city's noisy mix—sirens, the smell of asphalt, and sweet, greasy bakery treats. She knows the divide inside the Brotherhood isn't just talk—it's real, deep cracks no one, not even Kane, can fix. She traces the patterns, wondering—if Marcus rebels, if Ivan turns, if Kane falls, will the whole corrupt empire collapse? Or will a new leader rise, stronger and more dangerous?

This moment balances on the edge—a chance for change or disaster. She could break the story that topples giants, write her truth into the city's history. But seeing the men outside and remembering Jamie's fear, she knows she might start a war she can't control. The Brotherhood's crack is a fault line, and standing this close, she feels the shaking in her bones—both tempting and terrifying.

Trust is fraying. Past betrayals haunt every move. Mariel wants the big story but worries—what if she misjudges Marcus? What if uncovering the truth brings violence—against her sources, against her? Her drive burns strong, mixed with fear—a sharp blend like bitter espresso, a pain she knows well.

She closes her satchel, making sure every note and file is safe—the sum of risks taken and lines crossed. As the last light fades behind tall buildings, Mariel steps from the awning, her shoes splashing in a shallow puddle. The city's pulse hums around her, electric and wild. She gathers her courage and melts into the crowd—one woman loaded with secrets, drawn deeper into a dangerous game where shadows hide truth and danger.

The Courtroom Scene and Lucien's Entrance

Light filters through the stained glass windows, casting colorful patterns onto the marble floor—shades of gold, blue, and purple flicker as Lucien Blackwell walks. His shoes click quietly against the polished stone, making steady, sharp sounds. The whispers among the courtroom seats hush as he passes by. Reporters gather near the double doors, ready with their pens and cameras. They ask many eager questions, trying to dig into conspiracies, the mysterious Brotherhood, and rumors about a downfall. Camera flashes burst, catching the shine of Lucien's sharp navy suit. Every glance from the crowd is fixed on him, some eyes filled with hope, others with fear. He moves calmly through the courtroom, a place crowded with the ruined reputations of others.

The Manhattan courthouse has long been a symbol of power and drama, but this trial feels heavier, more serious than usual. Outside, the city buzzes with news. Electronic tickers flash the Brotherhood's name, TVs in store windows show experts guessing what might happen next, and protesters yell while security guards struggle to keep order. The Orion Brotherhood is no longer just a whispered rumor heard late at night—it is the center of the city's attention. Lucien looks at the crowd and the tall old building with its stone arches and carved details and knows this trial is not just an ending. It is a moment to uncover the truth. The courthouse walls, full of their own secrets over the years, are now quiet and tense, waiting for the truth to be revealed.

Preparations and Tensions Before the Trial

As Lucien walks deeper into the courthouse, he passes by groups of clerks and older lawyers. He catches his reflection fragmented in the glass panels along the hallway. Even though his heart beats steadily beneath his jacket, it feels hard and uneasy. He notices each small change—the judge arriving, which brings a hush over the room; the guards standing alert; the press ready to attack with new questions. The world shrinks down into a tight space filled with waiting and pressure. Beneath his calm exterior, his mind is busy—studying the charges, thinking about the weak points in the prosecution's case, and remembering Mariel's steady stare from the gallery.

Opposite him sits Damien Cross, silent but watchful. He rests his hands on the prosecutor's table and fixes his cold eyes on Lucien. The look is not friendly but a clear challenge. The judge, tired from years of hard decisions, sighs quietly and calls the room to order. The small noises—the benches scraping under shifting bodies, quick breathing—feel like the beginning of a great performance. Lucien wonders whether justice in this room will be real or just a show for the public.

Damien's Opening and Lucien's Strategy

Damien is the first to speak. His voice cuts through the quiet like a sharp blade. He speaks carefully and clearly, putting heavy charges on the table: racketeering, fraud, and criminal conspiracy. Damien calls the Brotherhood a harmful empire, deeply rooted in the city. He presents files filled with names and evidence, choosing his words like poison, always tying everything back to Lucien's group. Each sentence is a trap; every pause sends a sharp pain.

Lucien listens without showing any feelings. His jaw is tight, and his face is unreadable—a look that once made his enemies misjudge him as weaker. Inside, however, he is like a chess player thinking several moves ahead. He watches the speed of the fight, notices weaknesses in the prosecution's stories, and senses the jury's nervousness. He spots Mariel's tense figure taking notes quickly, her pen sharp and focused as if it could catch secrets floating in the air. The city's need for justice presses on everyone there, heavy and urgent.

When it is his turn, Lucien stands and speaks smoothly and confidently. His words fit the serious moment but show no fear. "Ladies and gentlemen of the jury," he says, "this place is for truth, not rumors. An accusation is not proof. Justice breaks easily when people want spectacle instead of facts." He does not deny much, instead turning questions back to the prosecution. He softens suspicion with careful reasoning, keeping the Brotherhood's true role hidden in shadows, inviting the jury to look but not find real evidence.

The Battle Between Prosecution and Defense

Damien grows more aggressive. His voice heats as he points out patterns and names people, calling Lucien's defense moves evasive and weak. Whenever Lucien tries to change the direction, Damien adds more fuel, revealing corruption that seems to reach deep into the city's foundations. Anger rises in the room. The air grows thick as both men fight to control the story, each word shaping what will come next for Manhattan.

The tension explodes when two of Damien's lawyers whisper plans quickly while Lucien raises an eyebrow in challenge. The judge's gavel thunders down, demanding silence. The sounds of the city seem to vanish, replaced by the noise inside the courtroom's old walls.

The judge warns firmly, "Any more chaos, and I will hold both sides in contempt."

A tense silence fills the room. The judge strikes the gavel again and pauses the trial for a moment. Chairs scrape quietly as people whisper, the quiet talks floating through the air. Lucien takes in the fading light and thinks about the cracks that might form once they begin again. The real battle is only just starting.

The Financial Expert and Uncovering the Numbers

The courtroom glows green and purple from the stained glass as silence stretches, filled with a dangerous sharpness. Cameras secretly record every moment. Lucien stands behind the defense table, cutting through the tension with his sharp presence. His navy suit is perfect, and every move seems practiced. He calls the Brotherhood's financial expert to testify, his voice calm and almost soothing, as if bringing peace before a storm.

The witness is a thin man with gray hair who shifts nervously under the watchful eyes of the courtroom and two news cameras. Lucien's questions are precise, like small surgical cuts through the truth hidden inside the numbers. "Can you explain which ledger entry—specifically February 22, column three—shows this isn't just a charitable donation? Why do you say this is money laundering?" Each time the witness stumbles or falters, Lucien presses gently with a low voice, leading him to slip into contradictions. What first seems like clear evidence becomes complex and confusing. A quiet respect grows in the room. Mariel's pen moves quickly, impressed by how Lucien explains and dismisses the charges as if wiping away chalk from a blackboard.

Damien's Evidence and the Increasing Pressure

At the prosecution's table, Damien leans forward, sleeves creaking as he moves. When Lucien sits down, Damien stands, holding a thick black folder that looks like a weapon. He speaks sharply to the judge: "Your Honor, we submit Exhibit G—bank records from Orion Holdings and emails legally obtained by subpoena. These are not just numbers. They show a hidden, planned scheme to hide money. Notice the recipient names, the secret transfers through fake companies in Zürich and Shanghai. Do not be fooled by tricks or guesses. The truth lies in these papers."

As the evidence is entered into the record, the whole room feels a wave of suspense. Damien flips pages and reads out emails filled with cold, business-like phrases such as "operational redundancy" and "risk mitigation." Sweat appears on the witness's forehead. Lucien watches Damien carefully, tapping his finger like a slow ticking clock.

In the press seats, Mariel sits focused among reporters, her notebook moving quickly. She looks for details the cameras miss. She catches Lucien giving a subtle hand signal—not to the witness, but to secret Brotherhood members. Behind him, two men exchange worried glances. She sees a Brotherhood ring glint quietly on a finger. Every little action she notes helps connect the public trial to hidden truths. Damien's voice rises more, accusing the Brotherhood more openly and threatening to reveal its influence over top city officials.

Mariel and Natalia's Secret Exchange

The judge calls a break, and Mariel slips away from the press crowd. She finds a quiet corner by a flickering snack machine, harsh light glowing nearby. Natalia Voss is there, her face hidden behind hair, gripping her phone tightly.

They exchange quick, secret messages full of meaning without words.

Mariel whispers, "He flagged column three again. It felt too planned."

Natalia replies, "I traced the wire from Zürich to Macon Avenue Trust. But there's a gap in time. Someone inside is covering this. It's more than a bookkeeping error."

"What about the last blackout?" asks Mariel.

Natalia's screen shows dates linked to important files. "Monday's file access matches a keycard used by someone in Judicial Records. I'll ask Ivy to check who was there during the suspicious emails." She watches a guard pass nearby.

"Be careful. This leak is dangerous."

Silence hangs between them, filled with shared risk. They are connected by late-night calls, by secrets, and trust in a city that often throws loyalty away.

Mariel's heart races as she looks toward the courthouse steps where sunlight glints on police barriers and reporters circle like predators. The Brotherhood's cover is breaking for everyone to see. Still, clinging to her notes, a sharp worry cuts through her hope: every answer they find brings new danger, breaking open the mask hiding the truth.

Yet with proof in hand and Natalia near, Mariel prepares herself. The moment of truth feels close, though the price might be higher than she had imagined.

Lucien's Challenge with the Forged Ledger

Bright noon sunlight pours through stained glass, filling the courtroom with yellow, blue, red, and gold hues that touch every face and add new drama. Everyone watches as Lucien Blackwell rises, sharp in his navy suit, standing clearly against the worn oak defense table. His face is steady, controlled, holding a manila folder that promises trouble.

"Your Honor," Lucien says smoothly, "I submit Exhibit F. I claim this ledger linking my client to the Orion Brotherhood is fake. I request a quick forensic check." He places the folder in front of the court clerk. The paper inside has a watermark that is just a little off, and the signature looks doubtful. Gasps spread through the courtroom. The jury seems to hold their breath.

Damien raises his hand, locking his jaw against rising anger. He grabs the document and scans it with eyes blazing. His anger is barely held back.

"This is a fake," Damien says, calm but sharp. "But the defense's trick won't work. Look at this second folder." He points to a thick stack of papers. "Forensics found a digital trail last night—metadata and timestamps don't match the dates. Clear signs of tampering. Your Honor, this is obstruction and an attempt to deceive the court. I demand an emergency hearing now."

Tension divides the two tables. Lawyers whisper plans quickly. Faces flush, knuckles tighten, sweat appears under collars. The judge hits the gavel three times; the sound echoes, scattering whispers.

In the gallery, Mariel crouches behind her laptop, white knuckles pressing keys. The light from the screen flickers on her face, eyes burning with urgency. She types: "Defense challenges prosecution—ledger's authenticity in doubt; forensic proof questioned; is truth really on trial?" She pauses, eyes fixed on Lucien. His jaw is tight, a faint scar glowing faintly in the colorful light as he stays silent under Damien's attack. Every move feels like it is planned, every feeling hidden. The mask never slips, but she senses a mental battle inside—how many moves does he have left and what cost will survival demand as the city watches?

Her mind races with what-ifs. If the evidence fails and the Brotherhood walks free, will her findings matter? Or will this be another story swallowed by the public's hunger for drama? She knows men like Lucien can bend rules and twist truths. Once, she thought exposing the truth meant power. Sitting there, heart pounding with every gavel strike, she wonders if the real maze isn't the ledger or testimony, but the invisible threats wrapping the courtroom tight.

Heated Exchanges and the Judge's Warning

A voice rises across the aisle, polite but sharp.

"Fake evidence, Lucien? Or have you finally ruined your own case just for show?"

"A man should know the difference between sabotage and strategy, Damien. That's what keeps some alive."

"No one survives forever. Not here."

"Is that a threat or a confession?"

The judge's patience ends. "Enough! This is a court of law, not a battlefield. Keep it down or I will hold you in contempt. Order! The record is sealed for review. No more outbursts."

The room grows thick with tension. Reporters scribble notes fast, jurors exchange worried looks, feeling a storm building in quiet silence. Mariel watches Lucien, his expression unreadable, but she sees a silent plea—a careful mental calculation. She wonders not just what he defends but who. Doubt grows inside her, mixing with duty. If she exposes him, will that destroy him? If she stays silent, is she part of another lie the city tells? She pictures headlines, both victory and loss, names erased, voices silenced.

Next to her, a woman whispers, "If this is justice, I fear it will lead to war."

Mariel's heart pounds as cold truth settles in: every word she types pulls her deeper into unknown dangers. Her phone buzzes with a secret warning. Natalia messages, "Be careful. They know there's a leak. Watch yourself."

For a moment, Mariel thinks about stepping back, wondering who she is if she does not move forward into the fire. Then the judge announces, "Court is in recess until further notice. All must stay nearby. Dismissed."

Lucien's eyes sweep the room, briefly locking with Mariel's. The moment burns with promise and threat. People file out as the city's fate breathes beneath the stained glass—truth and lies tangled together—and outside, the future waits, silent, hungry for whatever truth might survive.

A Rainy Evening in the Café

Rain trickles softly against the window, forming random shapes on the glass. Mariel watches them and thinks about the confusion she feels inside. The city has been stressful lately, so she looks for a quiet place to escape. Just outside Midtown, she finds a small café. Her raincoat is soaked through, with water running down the fabric, so she takes it off and hangs it over the back of her chair. It feels like setting down a heavy load she has been carrying.

Inside, the café is warm and cozy. The cold and wet world outside feels a long way away. The air smells of roasted coffee beans and sweet cinnamon pastries fresh from the oven. People talk quietly, careful not to break the calm atmosphere. This peaceful feeling is exactly what Mariel needs right now.

Soft, golden light fills the room. Glass globes hang from the ceiling, casting a gentle glow over each table. Shadows gather quietly in the corners, wrapping around cozy booths where customers lean close to share private conversations. Natalia waits at their usual table in a corner booth, holding a cup of warm tea that fogs up her glasses. Even though she looks tired, her smile is welcoming.

Mariel orders her usual black coffee—strong, with no sugar or cream. She sits down across from Natalia and feels a small relief at seeing a familiar face. Both women look worn out, carrying the heavy tiredness that comes from city life and chasing difficult dreams.

Talking About Fear and Trust

After a short silence, Natalia breaks the quiet by noticing that Mariel is late. She says this feels like a bad sign, which makes Mariel lower her voice. Mariel explains that people in the city know she is asking questions. She tells Natalia about meeting a source recently who got scared and stopped talking after she mentioned a secret group called the Brotherhood.

Natalia asks if Mariel pushed for more information, but Mariel says no. The man shut down quickly, his hands shaking, showing real fear. This was not just silence—it was a deep kind of fear that made Mariel uneasy.

As Mariel slowly stirs her coffee, careful not to spill the hot liquid, she admits to Natalia that the feeling of fear is spreading. It feels worse than just silence. Natalia warns her to be careful because rumors can be dangerous in the city. Mariel agrees. She shares how trapped she feels, like running through a maze someone else made. She worries that even people she trusts may be waiting to hurt her. Her jaw twitches, a sign that old worries are creeping back.

Looking around the quiet café, Mariel lowers her voice and talks about a colleague named Fallon. Fallon spread a rumor to exclude her. Mariel thought she had left betrayals behind, but they keep coming back. These betrayals make her feel isolated from the newsroom. No matter how hard she tries, she feels like an outsider in her own workplace.

Reaching across the table, Natalia takes Mariel's clenched fist in her hand. The touch is calm and firm, offering support without words. Natalia reminds Mariel that she is not alone—especially with her there beside her. She says Mariel has faced worse challenges before and always comes out stronger by trusting her instincts. She tells her she doesn't have to face this alone unless she wants to.

Mariel's thumb moves slowly under Natalia's hand. She is unsure if she should accept this kindness. Her instincts tell her not to trust so quickly, but Natalia's steady presence helps her feel a little safer. For a moment, Mariel thinks about years of secrets and betrayals. Even with those thoughts, the air feels calmer now. Natalia squeezes her hand and asks Mariel to remember this feeling—the strength that comes from support—for the hard times ahead. She promises to stay by her side no matter what rumors or trouble come.

Slowly, Mariel lets her guard down and exhales quietly, as if she remembers what it feels like to be truly seen. She offers a faint smile, but it does not fully reach her eyes. Outside, the rain slows down. Inside the café, two friends share a quiet moment when the world outside feels full of danger.

Alone in Her Apartment

When Mariel finally gets home, her apartment is quiet. The only sound is the soft humming of neon lights from outside, slipping through the windows and thin curtains. Her jeans are wet from the rain, with droplets sparkling faintly in the low light. She closes the door softly behind her, the quiet click marking the end of the day.

Outside, the city is still loud and restless. But inside, her apartment feels safe. It is a place where the chaos can't reach her. She quietly takes off her boots, places them aside, and hangs her raincoat on a chair near the door.

She moves over to the couch, a gray, worn-out piece of furniture surrounded by scattered papers and some houseplants. Kneeling on the cushions, she reaches under a bookshelf to pull out an old shoebox. The box looks soft and worn from many years of use. She blows off a thin layer of dust, then opens it carefully, holding it in her lap.

Though the city keeps moving fast outside, time seems thicker and slower inside this room. The box smells faintly of old ink and paper, with hints of coffee and wet cement from the street. Inside, Mariel finds photographs, notes, and press passes from protests and interviews long ago. Her thumb brushes gently over a photo showing two young women standing in a dorm hallway. They look full of hope and energy, ready to take on the world. Mariel's shoulders tense, and her chest feels heavy with memory.

She remembers when she was twenty, under a flickering dorm light, overhearing a friend say Mariel had shared a secret from a source but asked to keep it quiet. This was a betrayal. Mariel felt invisible and hurt. The next week, a rival publication broke the story first, and her friend avoided her. The trust between them broke, and silence covered what was once friendship.

Mariel stays on the photo for a long moment, her thumb touching the face of the friend who betrayed her. She closes her eyes, feeling the weight of that memory in her chest.

Another memory comes from December, in her family's apartment filled with spice smells and laughter. Mariel had just pitched her first big story and felt proud. Her cousin quietly encouraged her to keep going, to not let others push her out. But later, Mariel overheard her cousin laughing with others, calling her ambition a passing phase. The words hurt deeply, even if they came from a place of care. After hearing this, Mariel's confidence shrank, and she began to speak less.

These moments pile up like a wall around her heart. Mariel has learned to expect betrayal from strangers but also from people close to her. This armor protects her but also isolates her.

Leaning back on the couch, the weight of these memories presses down on her. Her laptop glows softly nearby, waiting for the stories she still struggles to tell. Frustration coils inside, sharp and painful, mixed with a deep need for connection.

Her walls keep her safe, but at a cost. They push away friendships and closeness. Every step toward trust feels risky and painful. This fear sits heavy in her chest, pressing down like a weight she can't shake. She knows that if she doesn't learn to open up, she will stay alone—brilliant but lonely.

Mariel stands and presses her forehead against the window. She watches city lights stretch out, steady and uncaring. Tomorrow might be different, but for tonight, she simply names her fear and refuses to give in.

An Encounter in the Newsroom

Night has fallen over the city, and the newsroom is quiet except for the steady hum of computers and the occasional whir of a printer. The room smells of ink and coffee, reminders of long work hours and tight deadlines.

Mariel sits at her desk, bent over a worn notepad covered with scattered notes and questions. She focuses deeply on her work, lost in thoughts about the stories she still needs to tell.

Suddenly, Lucien walks in. His steps are sharp and firm. He wears a dark, neat suit that stands out against the worn newsroom furniture. Passing an empty security station, he stops at Mariel's desk and quietly sets down a cup of takeout coffee—her usual order for late nights. The gesture seems friendly but careful, as if there is more between them than simple kindness.

Mariel looks up and narrows her eyes. She straightens in her chair but remains cautious. Lucien's gaze moves from her notepad to her face. Both know they share a complicated past, full of hard questions and untold stories.

He sits easily across from her, keeping his jacket buttoned and his collar shadowing his neck. The room is silent except for the soft buzz of lights and distant sounds from the city.

Mariel's fingers circle the warm coffee cup as Lucien speaks softly. He asks if she feels safe after the day's events—the courtroom chaos and everything else that happened. Mariel pauses, her voice tense. She says safety feels uncertain. She doesn't know who to trust now, not even him.

Lucien listens quietly, without anger or surprise. He admits he understands her suspicion. He shares his own past full of betrayal, starting when he was young. He explains that loyalty can be fragile in their world. Sometimes, hard choices must be made—even if that means betraying others.

Mariel says she doesn't want to live by those dark rules. She hopes to believe in something true, but every time hope breaks, it costs her deeply.

Lucien thinks for a moment, then places his hand gently over hers. His touch is warm and steady in the cold newsroom. Mariel does not pull away. For a moment, the noise of the city fades and is replaced by a quiet feeling of connection and cautious hope.

Then Lucien pulls back his hand, leaving a faint tremble behind. He stands, his face shadowed again. With a small nod, he leaves the room, disappearing into the empty newsroom.

Mariel holds her coffee, her pulse quickening as she watches flickering neon lights on her desk. Outside, the city is dark but alive. Dangers may still be gathering, but hope quietly lingers in the silence.

Web of Lies

City lights shine on the glass walls of Blackwell & Kane, casting moving shadows in Lucien's late-night office. Outside, Manhattan is alive with distant sirens and a single taxi horn mixing into the quiet inside. The air smells faintly of leather, burnt coffee, and the sharp scent of electronics working late. Lucien types quickly and precisely on his keyboard; the clicking is the only sound.

His screen displays spreadsheets with encrypted logs, intercepted messages, and internal notes from the Brotherhood's complex system. Numbers and codes form patterns that only he can understand. He notices some unusual entries—a data transfer at 3:08 a.m., another at 4:41 a.m., each marked with a small red flag. He zooms in, his eyes narrowing under the bright screen. Celeste's digital signature appears again and again, showing access at strange times from terminals used only by those deep in secret work.

Lucien leans in, focused, as he pulls up the full login history. Celeste's name glows on the screen—it feels personal but cold. He follows the strange login times: always after midnight, always from restricted rooms.

He remembers her as a child, fierce and secretive, and their last fight in this very office, voices sharp through the glass. Betrayal tastes bitter on his tongue. Has she turned against him? Has she destroyed the trust between them? The Brotherhood demands loyalty, and its fixer must never hesitate. Still, a painful memory lingers—a past of laughter between siblings now lost to secrets and unanswered questions.

Lucien grabs the encrypted phone, his thumb quick on the glass. He sends a brief message to Marcus: In the office. Now. Trouble. The device clicks softly as it returns to the desk.

He forces himself to look again—checking carefully to dispel doubt. Every piece is either proof or a weapon. Enough to shake the power they built together.

The door opens quietly, and Marcus steps in, his jaw tight with tension. He stands tall, but his eyes flick between the city outside and Lucien's unreadable expression.

"Have you seen anything strange lately? Communications, access points... anything off?" Lucien's voice is calm but sharp.

Marcus hesitates, glancing at the spreadsheets. "A few odd signals on the secure line. Some cache purges I couldn't track. I thought it was just maintenance."

"It's never just routine," Lucien replies without assigning blame.

Footsteps approach—the door opens again, and Elias Kane enters wearing a wet coat, his expression hard. Hands folded behind his back, he asks, "What's so urgent at this hour? You look like you've seen a ghost."

Lucien points to the glowing screen. "I'm reviewing logs. Data is moving the wrong way. Everything points to Celeste. I have time-stamps, access history, terminal IDs—no mistakes."

Elias frowns as he studies the data. Leaning close, his silver hair catching the light, he says, "Someone inside leadership is working against us. This isn't a small breach. It's a serious betrayal."

Marcus taps his knuckles nervously on the desk. "It could be a set-up. Digital credentials can be faked. Maybe she's being framed—you know how easy that is."

"Don't," Elias snaps. "Celeste's been disappearing for days, dodging questions, avoiding contact. She's always been careful, but not like this."

Lucien's stare intensifies. "Trust is gone until we find the truth. From now on, no one goes unnoticed."

No one argues. The quiet hum of electronics fills the room like a heavy silence.

Lucien sits back, pressing his fingers together until his knuckles turn white. Outside, city lights flicker. Marcus and Elias exchange uneasy looks—old bonds shaken by new doubts.

Lucien's chest tightens. Memories flash—Celeste laughing in a sunny Brooklyn apartment, retreating into shadows when she chose. He wonders which scars—his or hers—caused the deepest break.

What if Celeste isn't the only one compromised? What if the Brotherhood, sure of its power, is falling apart from within? Power is fragile. He sees the cracks—faces once trusted, from Elias to Marcus to distant leaders like Caius Drake and Silas Carver—each a possible enemy or victim. He imagines a city split by secrets, the end of what kept them safe. Pieces falling in a game that punishes the weak or the honest.

The east wind sweeps empty Manhattan streets as Lucien walks them, the city's heartbeat under puddles and neon lighting softening his footsteps. The Orion Club's back door waits beneath a flickering lamp. He lets himself in with a secret touch, and the door's heavy sound fades into the quiet behind velvet walls.

Inside, the room is full of secrets. Low lights cast soft glows on the polished wood. Smoke hangs lightly, barely stirred by an old fan, mixed with the smells of whiskey and metal. A row of men, all with marks of power, sit in shadowed chairs. Caius Drake, the youngest but coldest, crosses his arms, watching glass reflections more than faces. He observes but does not trust.

Lucien locks the door and places his tablet on a shiny black table. "No one leaves until this is finished," he says steadily, his voice as cold as the city fog outside. He brings up the breach report: logs with red flags marking Celeste Blackwell's access. The room holds its breath. Silas Carver sits half in shadow, hands folded, expression unreadable.

Elias Kane stands, his voice low but firm. "Gentlemen," he says, breaking the quiet, "we have a traitor here." His hard eyes find Lucien's, testing for weaknesses. Darius Hale, a surgeon known for walking away from broken things, leans forward with a steady jaw, taking in all the information but giving nothing back.

Lucien looks at each man. "Everyone linked to Celeste in the last two weeks is under watch. Silent, total surveillance. If anyone hesitates, someone else will step in. Marcus, start quiet interrogations. No rumors."

Marcus Reed squares his shoulders and nods, though his eyes are tight with suspicion, the lines on his face deepening.

"Anyone who leaks this gets exiled," Lucien continues, tapping his fingers on the glass. "Loyalty will be rewarded. Breaking trust will have consequences."

Elias signals for Lucien and three others—Caius, Silas, and Orion Vega, whose restless energy hints at rebellion and drink—to move to a darker corner. "Money won't fix this," Elias says quietly. "Some want immunity. Others fear. Let fear work. It binds tighter than gold."

Caius speaks softly, clearly. "If you push too hard, you risk chaos. These men will turn if they think no one is safe." Silas just nods, his silence heavy and full of meaning.

A soft tap: Marcus sends lieutenants down hidden hallways, signals flashing—a whisper, a note passed. Outside the paneled doors, tension thickens—people whisper in pairs, backs against decorated walls, voices dropping as suspects pass and doors close faster. Near the bar, a shaken hand spills whiskey on marble. Lucien takes it all in: spies watching spies, the Brotherhood closing tighter around its secrets.

Lucien and Elias step back, speaking quietly in the corner.

"This isn't just about Celeste," Lucien says, his voice tired and uneasy. "If trust breaks now—"

"It won't," Elias says firmly, gripping Lucien's arm. "I've seen empires fall from within. You do what you must. Cut anything that threatens us."

"So you'd cut your own—" Lucien's words stop in the dark.

"Anyone. Even you, if Manhattan needs it." A pause. "But I trust you still want to survive."

They hold each other's gaze—a battle between hope and despair, the weight of history between them.

In the hall, Marcus talks quietly with Darius while Orion listens nearby. "Do you want a list of what her allies touched? Club records, safe houses, digital entry points?" Marcus asks, low.

Darius looks at Orion, then back. "Be precise, not panicked. If we tear this apart, nothing holds us."

Orion raises his glass, smirking. "Or let it all burn and start fresh. Life's less boring then."

"Not my style," Marcus replies.

When Lucien returns, the room feels different. No laughter, just sideways looks and the soft scrape of glass on marble. Silas and Orion talk quietly, eyes growing wary where there was once trust. The club, once a refuge, now feels like a trap.

The Brotherhood's power comes from loyalty, promises deeper than skin and secrets locked under velvet and wood. But those same secrets, left unchecked, breed suspicion. Surveillance, rewards, threats, whispered rules—all tighten the empire, but the bond is fragile.

Lucien watches as the meeting breaks up, his senses sharp to every sound. The Brotherhood is alive tonight—broken, wild, and desperate to survive. Its life is silence. But Lucien knows that silence will one day shout.

Three floors up from the city's endless noise, Lucien Blackwell breathes the sharp air, electric with city lights. The cold cuts through his suit. He steps out onto the rooftop where the city's glow shapes his face. Glass towers shine in the dark, reflected on his polished shoes. The city below feels distant, its ambition rising like a promise or a threat.

The rooftop is quiet except for the soft hum of vents and a subway rumbling far below. Sirens sound faintly, and the smell of burnt food floats up from a late-night diner. The wind tastes like rain and old secrets.

Lucien's mind works fast. The Brotherhood's secrets are more than data—they are blood, power, and ruin, tied to the buildings of the city. The breach feels personal. The suspicion. Celeste's name and digital signs on stolen files. Is she the one behind it? Or just a pawn? Or worse—the real betrayer?

For years, he built his world on trust, only those with leverage, and planned for every betrayal. Now that certainty is gone. He stands on the edge of memories—Celeste's laughter in a Queens apartment, angry apologies that never healed the past.

His phone is cold in his hand—a secret device used only in emergencies. One ring, then another, until a rough voice answers faintly.

"Report," Lucien says, tight.

"You want surveillance on your sister? That's risky, even for you."

"I want all surveillance—digital and physical. No delays."

Static fills the line with distant city noise.

"You'll have it by morning. But if she runs—"

"I'll handle it."

The call ends. Lucien sighs and puts the phone away. He stands still, head bowed, eyes nearly closed. The Brotherhood demands full loyalty. No exceptions—not even family. But he imagines the other leaders: Elias, stern and experienced; Marcus, torn between duty and conscience; elders watching each other in smoky bars; Caius Drake, cool and calculating; Silas Carver, dark and dangerous.

He knows these men well. Power is the only currency here; love is a weakness. That's what makes tonight dangerous. Trust is rare; somewhere near, a skilled surgeon's reputation is stained—a warning that any empire can rot from within. Tomorrow, the old rules may end.

Lucien weighs his choices. He can expose Celeste to the Brotherhood's full force—bringing order but losing her forever. Or try to beat the evidence, risking everything if she's guilty. Or worse, if she's being used by enemies, by a leak they still hunt, or by their shared past. That doubt eats at him, darker than any fight.

His fingers tremble as he unclasp his wristwatch—the only gift from his sister he kept. The ticking is loud in the silence. He turns it over, then slips it back on. If he waits, and the Brotherhood falls, he loses more than his future. Redemption is not an option tonight. All he has is resolve.

He sends Celeste a short, secret message: Meet at dawn, safe house five. His thumb shakes, but the message sends hard like a verdict. No blame, just the threat that this meeting could change everything.

He stands on the roof as hours pass, arms crossed, breath freezing in the air. Below, the city doesn't sleep. Somewhere, people go about their quiet lives, unaware. The Brotherhood's trust is breaking, and the silence between buildings is sharp.

As dawn's cold light creeps over the skyline, Lucien stands ready—watching, serious, without softness. There's no time for doubt. The city waits. So does the reckoning.

The Gathering Storm

Midnight falls over Midtown's rough alleyways, glowing with bright neon lights. Graffiti of wolves and gang signs covers cracked walls, and the smell of fried food mixes with the fresh scent after rain. Tonight, these alleys are a battleground—a broken area where the city's hidden gangs fight to remain secret.

Two enforcers from the Orion Brotherhood, their faces half in shadow, rush past a flickering sign with a red snake symbol. Their boots splash through old puddles as car lights reflect off wet asphalt and broken glass. Suddenly, they run into a rival gang marked by bright green symbols. Voices shout in English and Spanish, and fists fly. Glass breaks as a bat swings with a sharp crack like gunfire. Alley cats scatter as the first punch lands. A bottle smashes against a shoulder. The strong smell of sweat, oil, and adrenaline fills the air. For a moment, the city seems to hold its breath.

Screams come from the alley as a gunshot rings out. People nearby—nurses off duty, club visitors—jump and run, some falling in fear. A backpack and a shoe lie alone on the street, shining beneath a flickering sign that flashes: EAT. DRINK. RUN. Red and blue police lights flash as sirens approach too late. Graffiti seems to watch, mocking the newcomers.

Inside a steel and glass building above the chaos, Lucien Blackwell remains calm. Shadows fall across his jaw as he reads urgent encrypted messages blinking on his screen. Video shows moving bodies, blood-stains, and a quick flash of a gun under bright neon lights. Text scrolls: attack at Midnight and West 39th, two down at Seventh, possible escalation. Lucien touches a scar on his jaw, thinking clearly. The city's fragile peace is breaking.

He makes a call.

"Marcus, we've been found out. Pull back from the West Side—double security at the Club and safe houses. Use Vega's route to retreat." His voice is cold and steady.

Marcus Reed replies quietly, urgently. "Got it. Lila heard chatter from Carver's crew—cover's blown at Chambers. Vega has tech locked down, but this might be the start."

Lucien thinks of Orion, daring and clever, able to reroute all feeds in Manhattan in minutes for fun. Of Silas Carver, who controls the news so the press follows his lead by morning. This is a game: Broth-erhood power—old blood, new money, hidden scars—against rivals who want chaos for their gain. Blow the balance, and the city forgets the rules. History shows the first to weaken loses badly.

The Brotherhood rules in shadows—working above the law but unseen, with power in courts and streets. Their rivals pry at their secrets, breaking alliances. Tonight, the streets are a chessboard with normal people caught in the moves. Lucien knows what must be done—cold logic and violence where the law can't reach. He tightens control, always fixing problems. But outside, blood shines, and trust is rare and expensive.

He ends the call. The city lights flicker over his desk—a green glow from Orion's tool, a flash of Seraphina's laughter from a club window, a whisper of distant rain like a promise Lila made in a far hospital. But for Lucien, feelings are a danger. His sharp reflection looks back.

In the alley, the fight is over. Police cars arrive with tires hissing. Mariel Dawson crouches near a dumpster, camera ready, knees touching broken glass and sticky puddles. Cold bites her cheeks. She smells gunpowder, burnt food, and blood. She takes pictures: a bullet shell in a gutter, a bloodied shoe near trash, the pale face of a shocked vendor smoking nervously.

Her voice is steady even though her heart races. "What did you see?"

The vendor coughs, his voice rough. "Masks, many—one threw a bottle, then the tall one—he dragged someone behind crates. Like he was saving him, not finishing it. Do you really want to print this?"

"Someone has to."

She writes fast, careful, noting his pain beneath his brave voice. Blue lights get closer, shining urgently. Sirens press around her, pushing her forward. Mariel holds her camera tight, evidence hidden deep in her jacket. She watches the police set up barriers and shout orders.

A voice yells, "Miss, get back! This is an active crime scene!"

Mariel moves aside, blending with fleeing club visitors. She steps through a puddle shining with broken neon lights—rainbow colors under her boots. Her mouth tastes of adrenaline and city smoke as she slips away before the police close off the alley, disappearing into the restless city.

Upstairs, Lucien watches as Manhattan's fragile order shakes. He feels the weight: power balanced on the edge of violence, a secret empire one mistake from falling apart. The Midnight Streets below still burn—tonight's fight is just a warning of the larger war coming.

The café holds on to the last hours of night—inside glowing with dull gold from broken lights. The air smells of burnt espresso and old linoleum, cutting through the faint city breeze slipping under the door. Mariel sits quietly, grounding herself in the familiar roughness as she presses into a sticky vinyl booth. The light from her laptop spreads over messy notes. Her camera bag rests beside her, still dirty from the alley, with a faint bloodstain from the Midnight Streets.

The bell above the door rings. Detective Samuel Graves enters, blocking the early morning light. He doesn't look around; he knows where Mariel will be. He moves smoothly up to the counter, orders black coffee in a calm, clear voice. Coins drop onto the counter. Then he sits across from Mariel, dropping his broad shoulders back, nodding once like sealing a quiet deal.

Between them is a heavy silence. Graves's coffee arrives hot, but his hand, not his eyes, slides a thick folder onto her knee. His hands are rough, scarred, nails short. Mariel doesn't open the folder yet; she studies him instead, noting his face, jaw, and quick breath.

He keeps his fingers on the folder and leans in slightly. "You were at the scene on 47th?" he asks. His voice is casual but leaves a sharp edge, daring her to say more.

"I was there," Mariel says, taking her cold, untouched coffee. "After the shooting. I have interviews and photos. You know why I'm here."

A quick twitch of his mouth disappears fast. "My team heard otherwise. Thought you were front row when it started."

She ignores it, watching his right hand rest on a napkin. He seems to notice her stare and curls his fingers.

"This is from tonight," he says softly, carefully, "and two witness reports. Off the record. This isn't just gangs fighting. Someone's behind this, picking targets in the Brotherhood." His dark eyes meet hers. "Higher-ups are watching."

Mariel pulls the folder closer. Its rough cover crackles slightly, like her own nerves. She peeks inside: printed pages, photos from grainy security cameras—gang shadows, Brotherhood signs barely hidden, faces she knows and some she doesn't. Graves's notes snake through the margins: names, patterns, places.

If this is a trap, it's detailed. But if it's real…

He lowers his head, voice tight. "They want this city broken, Ms. Dawson." His lip twitches—not a smile but something close. "No matter what you think about the Brotherhood or Lucien Blackwell—there are worse dangers. Trust me."

Trust. The word hits hard. Mariel's gut tightens—she's been betrayed before, left with scars that never go away. Nights in police stations, a mentor's empty promises, the sound of footsteps after being thrown under every political bus. She wants a chance, proof, but her instincts scream danger.

She watches Graves closely: his thumb rolling over a knuckle, his raised eyebrow when she stays silent.

She leans in, careful to match his low tone. "If we work together, my rules. Encrypted channels—mine, not yours. Share as little as possible. We're both targets if anyone's watching. And don't tell me no one's watching."

He nods slowly, reluctantly. He slides an old, secure phone her way. Their hands touch briefly. "Trust is dangerous. Choose wrong, you end up dead—or worse. That badge doesn't make me safe either."

"Noted." She puts the phone and folder away. "Then don't expect me to work for free."

"Wouldn't think of it."

Neither softens.

Graves picks up his empty cup, stands with a grunt and a newspaper under one arm. Mariel watches the paper, its headline still unclear. She picks at a tear in the folder, breathing in the mix of wet metal and burnt coffee. The secrets in her hands feel like a poised snake, every name and time sharp on her skin.

Her mind races—imagining what Caius Drake, a billionaire controlling chaos from his glass tower, would think. Or Darius Hale, cold and distant, breaking down threats like surgeries. Even Orion Vega's reckless ghost seems to linger, and Silas Carver's whispered name chills the city's veins.

Police sirens fade in the distance. Graves is gone. Mariel stays with the folder, alone except for the city closing in, holding the storm of secrets she just invited.

Lucien opens the last security door, coldly leading Mariel, Natalia Voss, and two Brotherhood lieutenants into the heart of the Orion Club. Heavy velvet curtains block out the city, silencing the shouts and sirens behind thick glass. Inside, the world shrinks to close bodies, the smoky smell of old whiskey, and soft voices behind wooden walls. Even the dark wood furniture reflects only faint faces, shadows of doubt and plans.

The group settles in the club's hidden lounge. Leather chairs accept them cold and firm. Lucien signals for quiet. Mariel feels the two lieutenants' eyes—one pale and scarred, one dark and quiet—and meets Lucien's steady gaze. Her heart beats deep under the rain hitting stained glass. Natalia, no drama, shows their evidence—their weapons are truth, not bullets: a battered folder, worn by street dirt and rain; a glowing tablet with Ivy Thompson's maps showing the city's underground paths.

Natalia lines up the photos—one after another: puddles with neon splashes, bruised alleyways, bullet casings among old party flyers. She points to timelines marked in red. "See the pattern? This isn't random. Every fight and attack has a purpose. Someone is tracking us."

Mariel speaks quietly, sure. "These are warnings. Someone is closing the trap—not just on you." She looks at Lucien, holding back questions or blame. "What you want hidden, someone else wants to expose."

Lucien's look is sharp but respectful. "Show me."

Natalia hands over the tablet. Ivy's map lights up with colored points—Midnight Streets, Cherry Lane, several Brotherhood buildings circled like targets. Club lights flicker as Lucien's eyes narrow, making Mariel feel the tension in the room.

Marcus Reed arrives, broad and tense, his jacket smelling of rain and cold metal. "Bad night." He nods to Lucien, then to Mariel and Natalia, alert as a street cat. Another Brotherhood man stands silent by the door, scanning the shadows.

Marcus puts a thumb drive on the table. "Arrest records, chats, delivery lists—too neat. Half these people are fake. The crowd on Cherry Lane didn't miss anything." He looks at Mariel without blinking. "Want protection? You follow our rules, not the NYPD's."

A hot feeling rises in Mariel's neck. Marcus's words are both a threat and an offer. She wonders if he's honest or just calculating. "I'm not your enemy," she says quietly, "but I'm not your shield either."

The group dives into serious talk. Safe houses, secret money accounts online, tracking leaks, secret message drops. Natalia, gripping her phone, suggests a controlled leak—enough to scare outside groups but not burn the Club. The silent lieutenant thinks over losses. Lucien watches them all, deciding who's safe and who would be marked if things go wrong.

Mariel catches Marcus's gaze—a quiet challenge under the storm's noise. "If this truce falls apart, it won't be because of me," she says. Marcus nods reluctantly. Their handshake is stiff, cold fingers meeting hard palms. No one bows, but something shifts—a shared need to survive, if not trust.

As tasks are shared, Ivy's name appears on their secure chat. "Channels open. Can't vouch after tonight. Watch yourselves," she writes, her presence ghostly among shadows. The plan unfolds carefully—coded messages, planned escapes, a timeline to buy them some t ime.

The storm shakes the glass again, scattering light across Lucien's face. He watches Mariel closely, looking for cracks in her will. This is a tense pause before more conflict. Beneath the city, people like Caius Drake, Darius Hale, Orion Vega, and Silas Carver move secret pieces in a dangerous game no one fully sees yet.

One by one, the group leaves into the night, boots echoing on marble floors toward new storms. Lucien stays at the door. Mariel turns, her heart pounding with a question she won't say. Their eyes meet, sharing silent understanding: tonight's peace may win a battle, but it has changed all the rules of the war.

Unseen Truths

The elevator opens with a muted chime, the sound swallowed by the plush, midnight-blue hush of Lucien's skyscraper. Mariel steps out, drawn deeper into the hall where light barely bleeds from frosted sconces. Her phone—still warm from staccato texts and a recent call with Natalia—feels too heavy in her hand. The corridor is bone-quiet. On her left, a museum-grade abstract looms, echoing disjointed shadows that flicker as she moves. Ahead, at the end, the penthouse door waits like a boundary between worlds, matte black and guarded by a discreet security plate. She hesitates for a beat, pressing her palm flat over her fluttering heart. Her reflection stares back in the brass number, eyes too wide, hair rumpled with rain from the cab r ide.

On the other side, Lucien opens the door before she can knock, wordless, his gaze a blade of exhaustion. His suit jacket is slung somewhere out of sight. He's wearing a dark henley and slate-colored trousers, his feet bare on the cool marble. There's a shadow of stubble along his jaw, a smudge below one eye like a bruise.

"Come in," he says, his voice rougher than usual yet controlled, drawing her inside and closing the door with a soft, definitive click.

City light spills through uncurtained, floor-to-ceiling windows, scattering the penthouse in sharp ribbons of silver and neon. The living room smells faintly of ink, fine whiskey, and the ozone tang of rain on glass. Mariel slips out of her shoes, tension thrumming in her shoulders, and crosses over the thick rug toward where Lucien stands by an onyx bar. He pours two fingers of whiskey, the liquid catching the blue-red pulse of distant sirens.

He gestures for her to sit—a velvet armchair facing the low table, across from him, an equal distance from isolation and intimacy.

He hands her the glass, then finally sits, his body folded in on itself more than she's ever seen. Silence grows thick as dusk. Only the ambient city—horns, wind battering high glass, the animal growl of an unseen train—offers any sound.

Lucien breaks the silence first. "Chaos is a strange teacher," he murmurs, tracing the rim of his glass with one careful finger. "The past few days... Brotherhood's unraveling. Old certainties start to rot when the foundation cracks beneath you."

Mariel stares into the amber whirl, her mouth prickling with the bright burn of fear. Her throat is tight. Saying nothing would be easiest, but something inside tips.

"I keep thinking I can handle this." Her voice wavers, then settles into a steadier register. "But after what happened on 52nd—the gunshots, my friends scattered—I realized... I might have broken something we can't put back. I can't stop replaying Ivy's call, the way Natalia sounded when she told me it wasn't safe to go home. I'm afraid, not just for me. If anything happens to them—to my family—" She breaks off, breathing in whiskey fumes and city ozone, blinking fiercely against tears.

Lucien listens, surprisingly still. For once, the sharpness of his presence is blunted, as if he's folded inward to some unsafe music. His thumb brushes absently over his wristwatch, the cold steel catching thin light.

"I know that fear," he says, his voice softer, dark with an edge of confession. "You put faith in your own people—and then remember the only thing more dangerous than an enemy is a friend with secrets. I thought I was untouchable, once. Now every shadow in this city feels like a blade at my back."

She wants to flinch at the openness—wants to scoff at him, the fixer in his glass fortress, daring to talk about fear. Still, something raw and old tugs at her; the memory of a different mentor, trust shattered by a lie, sharp as broken glass. Mariel swallows and leans forward.

"You just trust no one? That's how you live? Doesn't it wear you down?"

His lips press together in a humorless smile. "I trust outcomes. Not intentions. Safer that way."

She brushes the back of her hand across her eyes, her knuckles tight. For a long, impossible moment, she hesitates, then simply reaches for him, her palm laying gently over his.

The contact is a livewire—heat, pulse, memory. Lucien's eyes close as if he might let himself fall through the quiet, just for a breath.

But only a breath. He lifts her hand away, his fingers cool, lingering longer than they should.

In the stillness, words spin between them, barbed and trembling.

Lucien rests his whiskey on the table. "We're burning each other alive, Dawson. Maybe... maybe we try something else," he says, the casual mask discarded, his voice nearly hushed. "We track who's tearing at both our worlds. We aim at the threats—not each other."

She hears her heartbeat, feels the static between want and suspicion, hope and memory. There's too much risk. But also, something humming with fragile possibility.

Mariel nods once, wary yet unable to pretend she doesn't want this—just for tonight, just one inch closer to trust.

Outside, the city wind keens against the glass, rattling it faintly—a wild, midnight lament for secrets neither of them fully own. They sit, two adversaries balanced on the precipice of alliance, shadows stretching long and uncertain as the night.

Lucien leads Mariel down a narrow hallway. The floor vibrates faintly under their footsteps, the city's pulse transmitting through steel and glass. The study waits at the end, walled mostly in glass—the midnight skyline fractured by reflections of their shapes, their secrets. The lights are dim, so the city's glow edges everything in shadow. Chill air tastes of old books, whiskey, and the ozone tinge of rain not yet fallen.

She drops her messenger bag beside a gleaming steel desk, the metal cold beneath her palms as she peels back folders. Photos scatter onto the surface—crime scenes lit in harsh flash, evidence tags glowing fluorescent, close-ups of coded graffiti left in the wake of a violence that ripples out in circles she once believed were predictable. The whirr of the city fades beneath the page shuffle, the low hum of a security camera somewhere above.

Lucien is silent behind her, his shadow brushing the edge of her vision. She feels the scrutiny before she hears him move. There is a subtle click as he unlocks a drawer, his movements precise and practiced. She watches his hand—a brief tremor betraying how even fixers can come undone.

He draws forth coded ledgers bound in black, slips of parchment stitched into the spines, and a sheaf of weathered correspondence, some scrawled in meticulous cipher, some in the hurried hand of someone who feared time was up. He places them on the desk with a soft thud, then opens a battered folder marked with an unfamiliar emblem. It smells faintly of burnt paper and something acrid, like secrets kept too long.

She lays out printed screenshots—encrypted chats, shell company links, payment traces. Newspaper clippings smudged with ink and coffee. She keeps a photo at the center: a map of intersecting lines over Manhattan, each intersection a night when blood seeped into concrete and the headlines screamed.

Lucien leans over her shoulder, his finger tracing a path between Hell's Kitchen and the Upper East Side. "You're missing this axis." His voice is low, words measured, and she resists the urge to pull away—wants, impossibly, to lean in.

She fights the tremor in her throat. "Then show me." Her own voice surprises her—steady, with only the faintest rasp betraying exhaustion.

He slides her notes aside, laying his own intelligence bare. "My sources intercepted this." He flicks a coded document toward her, his brows drawn tight. "The assaults weren't wild. They were precise—coordinated hits meant as signals, not warnings. There's no chaos. There's choreography."

For a moment, she bristles at the correction, at the implication she's out of her depth. Trust isn't natural here. Not with him. Her muscles coil with remembered lessons—never let a lion near an open wound.

Their hands nearly touch as they flatten a blueprint of the city, fingers grazing the same outline of a hidden club around Murray Hill. His palm is warm; hers is cold from the printouts. She tries to ignore the static that lances up her arm.

She says, "Ivy can crack the surveillance feeds near this site. Natalia still has a source at the city planning office—their records have been tampered with, but she's cautious." She watches Lucien weigh each name, like chess pieces with hidden blades.

He counters, "Two Brotherhood insiders are already wavering. Marcus Reed—he's loyal but doubting, and Celeste... well, my sister's alliances are her own. We can't force trust. We can... persuade it, if we move carefully."

Lightning flickers over Queens. Framed by the city's unrest, their collaboration sharpens, dialogue darting from clipped to incendiary. His caution is glacial, shaped by losses he's catalogued but never confessed. She presses, risking more: "If we don't warn certain people now, we're handing the instigators a massacre. Lauren can leak to the media without naming names. Detective Graves owes me for last spring—he'll know when to keep evidence in his desk drawer."

He cuts in, his voice icy. "You leak and you damn them. Every time the wrong file lands in the wrong inbox, another corpse shows up. I won't bury more bodies for the sake of half-truths. We can't protect everyone."

She meets his gaze, her chin raised. "Then at least let us protect the ones who matter." Their words dart and scrape, but beneath the eruption—a low symphony of understanding, a grudging respect that is all the more dangerous for its honesty.

He offers a compromise, and she senses it in the tightening of his jaw, the guarded hope in his eyes. "We set a trap. Feed them a trail, watch who bites. I'll spin the Brotherhood's web tighter. You shield your friends. But we don't share everything. Not yet."

A pause. Then, "Deal," she murmurs.

Their hands meet in a handshake meant to be businesslike, but neither is in any rush to let go. The contact lingers—a flare of warmth, a silent dare, a shared admission that, for tonight, their war is on hold.

He steps back first, folding into shadow. She exhales, finally, and moves to the window, pressing her forehead to the cool glass. Across the city, the lights of rival empires flicker; far below, a single yellow cab cuts through the rain-slicked street—a reminder of other wars, other survivors, of new storms already gathering.

For the first time, she wonders—not can she trust him, but can she trust herself not to want what trust might bring.

Lucien stands beneath the low, golden light of the penthouse foyer, the city's night pulsing beyond glass and steel. A trail of whiskey lingers on his tongue, mingling with the memory of Mariel's hand pressed briefly—too briefly—over his own. Now, as they hover in this threshold space, Lucien senses the crackle of momentum between risk and surrender. His tailored shirt is open at the throat, sleeves pushed carelessly up his arms, as if the armor of his usual world has been peeled off, layer by reluctant layer.

He gestures toward the door, then hesitates. "I should warn you—trust isn't something I offer. Not to anyone. Definitely not to you. Not after tonight, not after everything... but something's changed." His voice is low—measured, yet raw at the edges, each syllable edged with exhaustion and a strange, furtive hope.

Rain-spattered wind rattles the windows high above Manhattan, unsettled and hungry. Mariel's fingers rest on the cold steel door handle. Her hair—still damp from the late night—frames her face, throwing shadows beneath her jaw. The air is tense with possibility; her breath hitches before she finds words. In her silence, she seems on the verge of flight, but something holds her rooted just inside his sanctuary.

He watches her profile catch in the city's diffused blue light, alert for the tell of emotion: the slight flinch at his words, her gaze flicking up, seeking meaning like a bloodhound on the scent. In this quiet, Lucien's composure falters. Years of Brotherhood training caution him—never show the wound, never drop your guard. Yet, tonight, with the world outside warring and the darkness pressing close, he finds himself lowering the walls, if only for a heartbeat.

"You're not the only one who's been burned," he says quietly.

Mariel's knuckles whiten, but she doesn't run. If anything, she leans into the moment, tension dancing across her posture. She looks back at Lucien, the question clear: Is this real? Is he dangerous? The answer, of course, is both. Her pulse beats visibly along her neck.

Lucien's mind whirls with specters—visions sharper than streetlight refracted on rain-slick glass. He sees, impossibly, a Manhattan where the Brotherhood's shadow recedes and the two of them stand unmasked, allies—perhaps more. He feels the allure of that world: Mariel laughing, warm, forging stories not meant for ruin, but for building something new. For an instant, he wonders if redemption is possible, if the tangled bloodlines and grim loyalties that defined him could unspool into softer threads. But he knows better—knows wounds this deep rarely heal clean.

He sees, too, the other path: Mariel's investigation laid bare, headlines blazing with Brotherhood crimes, trust gutted, the city's elite in free fall. He imagines himself alone in ruthless survival, forced to silence her or be destroyed by her truth. In that future, the echo of her voice lingers only as a challenge, a regret that stings sharper than a knife to the gut.

Between those futures, Lucien stands paralyzed—yearning for connection, but honed by betrayal. He remembers what he learned from Elias Kane: trust is a currency, and the world only respects those who hoard it. But the faint pressure of Mariel's hand earlier, the vulnerability in her voice, has upended that calculation.

He tries to pin the emotion, to find language for it, but comes up empty.

Their gazes lock across the threshold. Lucien's eyes—obsidian, almost reflective—hold questions he never dares ask. Mariel's are wide, uncertain, reflecting city lights and storm-lit hope. For a moment, the distance between them is charged—neither adversary nor ally, but something twisted and rare, born of danger.

She turns the handle. "If I walk away, nothing changes," she says, her voice barely above a whisper. "You'll go back to your empire. I'll chase a story the world's too afraid to hear."

Lucien's mouth quirks, bitter and soft all at once. "And if you stay?"

"Then we both risk what little we haven't yet lost."

For a long beat, the foyer is silent but for the distant wail of a siren and the rush of city wind. The air smells of ozone and expensive cologne, a memory of rain and lightning hanging between them.

Finally, Mariel pulls open the door. Cool air sweeps in, carrying the restless breath of urban night. Her heels click softly down the marble corridor. She turns, once, casting a look back through the narrowing slice of light. Lucien stands framed in gold and shadow, still—watching, wary, impossibly open.

As the door closes behind her, Lucien remains unmoving, his heart drumming wild in his chest. For an instant, he lets himself imagine how easily this moment could have fractured: an argument, a confession, a desperate plea. He wonders—what would it mean to lay down his weapons, to offer vulnerability, to trust Mariel and let her see the pieces of himself he's hidden even from the Brotherhood?

A memory flickers—Caius Drake's icy detachment at the club, Darius Hale's cold refusal to yield emotion, Silas Carver lurking in shadow, always scheming. Lucien has known all their faces, every shade of armor, every mile of distance between hope and annihilation. Yet it is this, a woman in the corridor, a final locked glance, that cleaves him open.

In the silent echo of Mariel's departure, Lucien lets himself dwell—just briefly—in that speculative, dangerous hope.

The elevator chimes, carrying her away into the city where, somewhere, others like Darius and Lila fight their own impossible tides. The world outside is vast, cruel, maybe just wild enough to offer second chances. For Lucien Blackwell, the cost of hope might be everything.

Betrayal Unmasked

The elevator emits a low, steady noise that vibrates through Celeste Blackwell's body. She stands near the edge of the bright city lights, with Manhattan's quiet night outside the concrete walls. The empty parking garage stretches before her, dark with broken lights flickering. Her boots make sounds on the oily floor as she walks carefully. The sharp smell of ozone and car exhaust fills the air, matching the nervous energy inside her.

She stops to look around. Security cameras flash red lights from metal poles, but her heart rate slows; she knows every angle, has blurred most camera feeds, and slipped through a system she helped create. In the far corner, a shape leans into the shadows—a person dressed entirely in black, their face hidden under a hat, as quiet as the restless city.

Celeste moves closer, breathing softly, holding a folder tightly against her chest—the edges worn from nervous fingers, full of secrets she can't risk keeping. The other person's hand reaches out, pale and waiting. No words are spoken as they exchange something: the soft

sound of paper, a quiet pact that makes the hairs on her neck stand up
.

Her voice is low, cutting through the smells of exhaust and wet rain. "The Brotherhood's weak points are clear. Their security is two weeks behind on digital protection. Lucien's too busy fixing Kane's mess. He's not watching what's hidden." She looks up, her eyes wide like a night animal's, searching for any hint of lying. "The council is splitting. Someone wants a vote—someone from outside, maybe Silas Carver's group." The name carries weight, reflecting the power Silas has, known in secret meetings and formal offices.

The figure nods silently and puts the folder into a worn bag. No questions, just a soft step away. Celeste feels a shiver, as if the city itself is listening.

She blends into the fluorescent light, fear souring her mouth. She leaves, and the city's energy grows—a tide of business and ambition rising above these underground tombs. The wet asphalt shines from the rain, the air thick and smelling of diesel. Outside the Orion Club, sharply dressed people gather under the entryway—some laughing, some calm and patient, their faces lit by gold and blue streetlights. She waits, hiding behind a column, watching every face closely. There is no sign of Lucien's usual proud look—his presence would have brought the crowd closer, sharing loyalty and suspicion.

She moves close, blending with a group of nervous young members. Her hand grips a heavier folder now, pages wrapped in plain manila paper. Inside: access logs, money records, encrypted orders—the kind Lucien hides, the kind that could buy freedom or destroy lives. She nods to a distracted guard and slips down a side hall, past velvet ropes and paintings, then out unnoticed into a narrow alley filled with rain runoff and city secrets.

The cold wind brushes her cheek, cooling her panic. Memories come in shards:

A night three years ago—Lucien laughing, holding a whiskey glass, urging her to trust Kane's plan. Her heart raced; she let him see it, making him think her loyalty was unbreakable.

Another memory—her fingers moving over server codes, blocking security cameras before Kane's private meeting. Damien Cross paced outside, smart but not smart enough to catch her trick.

Snatches of conversation: Lucien's voice, low and filled with hidden care. "You'd tell me if something was wrong." She had smiled, staying silent. Had she ever warned him that truth is rare and kept carefully in this world?

She built her reputation in small moves: planting doubt in trusted ears, faking leaks to shift suspicion, while gaining trust by sharing pieces of her pain with Lucien. The Brotherhood trusted those who shared their wounds. She had plenty. The pain of betrayal is sharp against old wounds—ones Lucien never saw, earned before her first code was cracked or her first lie told.

Now, as the city quiets, she stands under a dull streetlight. A strong wind rises from the Hudson, making her eyes sting. Across the street, the Orion Club's doors open, and Lucien steps out—always perfect, his gaze scanning the dark, tight with mistrust. He stops, maybe sensing her, but the night is full of secrets.

Celeste tightens her grip. Her face hardens, her jaw clenched so tightly it hurts. Losing trust is heavy in her stomach, but the folder burns in her hand—hope for justice, something clean in a world full of hidden deals. She watches Lucien get into a waiting car, rain turning the city into shining jewels, then fades into the shadows, another ghost in Manhattan's restless heart.

Lucien sits alone in a large conference room, the lights low and soft. Outside the tall glass windows, the city looks bruised under the midnight rain. Manhattan's streets glow with red taillights and neon signs; inside, only the hum of air control and the quiet storm sounds. Leather creaks quietly as he moves, the room feeling like it's holding its breath.

He looks at the folder on the dark table—its sharp corners casting uneasy shadows. The storm outside grows louder, rain running down the glass. Lucien checks his phone again. At this hour, messages mean threats, not help: one from Caius Drake about a frozen secret asset, another from Silas Carver's media team about a rumor tied to a surgeon's foundation. The Orion Club's power reaches far, but here in this empty room, Lucien feels the world closing in.

The elevator's sound breaks the quiet. Celeste steps in, rain dripping from her slick hair, her coat hanging heavy. She says nothing, but the smell of cold rain and city dirt follows her. A flash of an old scar on her neck, half-remembered fights and secrets, pulls at him in a way his tough public image can't hide.

He gestures silently to the chair across from him. She closes the door softly.

He slides the folder with proof of betrayal across the table. Next, he lays out a set of photos: Celeste entering and leaving the Orion Club's most guarded rooms, caught by hidden cameras. She touches the folder's edges but keeps looking at him.

"Want to explain," Lucien says, his voice sharp, "why my sister is a shadow on our own cameras?"

Her lips part, breath catching—not guilt, just pause. "We both see the Brotherhood is sick, Lucien. You know it." She looks at the rain on the glass, defiant. "New players are here. Forces the old guard misses or ignores. You think I wanted this?"

Lucien's hands tighten on a file. The worst betrayal he's known was when a trusted club lawyer sold them out to federal agents. Trust is like money—easy to fake. But this—his own blood breaking ranks—hurts deeper than any court betrayal.

He stands and walks around the table, thunder rolling outside. Each step is careful, almost like a ceremony. Memories come: Celeste smiling after hacking a school system; how she slipped past tighter security than any child should, then returned with keys no one noticed missing.

Her voice softens as he nears. "I did what I had to. Things are changing—Elias Kane acts like a king, but the ground's shifting. Someone's fighting for power, ready to burn us all."

He stands over her, rain reflections on the glass, his face unreadable except for a vein pulsing at his jaw. "You could have come to me. Instead, you shared our secrets with strangers. You put the Club, the Brotherhood, and me in danger. If you wanted out, I could have protected you my way." His words cut between blame and pain, a warning she knows well.

"Your way?" Her bitter laugh breaks through the rain and memories. "You hide the truth, Lucien. Whatever's coming, you can't fight it with papers and threats."

"So you betray us? Give them a map to our weaknesses?" His control is about to break. He wants to reach out to hold her but stops himself.

"Better a traitor than a pawn." Celeste meets his eyes. "They're coming for all of us—me, you. I won't watch the next wave hit, not after Cassel, not after the Club ruined Darius Hale's reputation, or set Elara as bait for Orion's revenge." Her words fall like glass between them.

He stares, fears leaking through his doubts. Can he trust anyone now? Or is this life just a mask hiding knives? The Brotherhood made him for nights like this: to protect power, crush enemies, even if those enemies are family. He's lost friends and lovers to secrets and survival. Now, with thunder overhead, he wonders—not if he'll destroy her, but if he'll survive it.

Her face is pale but firm as she moves past him. They spin apart, pulled away.

Finally, Celeste slips out, her steps disappearing into the carpet and storm. Lucien stays, the folder open on the table, his hands shaking to hold it together. Outside, the city flashes with light and shadow—a place where tonight, betrayal cuts deeper than the rain.

Mariel's hands feel cold under the blue light of her laptop in the empty newsroom. The clock shows nearly three. Rain taps on the window. Old headlines, yellowed and curling, watch from boards—a silent mix of wins and losses. Her story is not printed yet. Her heart beats fast.

Her phone vibrates on the desk. She looks down; it's an old phone with a small heart sticker peeling at the corner. Unknown number. The preview shows: Chinatown alley. 23 Mott Street. Brotherhood. Tonight. Want the truth? Move now.

A chill goes through her chest, colder than the room air. She stands, looks out at the quiet city, then grabs her bag, slipping in two notebooks and her press badge. Her knuckles turn white as she hits the dirty elevator button, adrenaline rushing.

Outside, the air is heavy with city dirt and the smell of fried food from a closed cart. Cabs splash through puddles, tires spraying water.

She walks fast, heart pounding, boots stepping around shiny gutters and trash lit by street lamps. Every step sharpens her senses, reminding her of all the late-night stakeouts that went wrong—times when her gut told her to step left just before violence hit. Years of barely escaping danger have made her careful. Sometimes it's enough. Sometimes it isn't.

At this hour, Chinatown glows with red lantern light on wet concrete. Steam rises from a manhole near an alley, neon signs glowing at the entrance, puddles shining on the ground. She slips into the narrow path, smelling the sourness of spoiled vegetables and incense. Her footsteps sound like secrets she tries to swallow.

Trash bins stand in piles—onion skins, fortune cookie wrappers, wilted lily roots. She crouches behind them, her knees wet and cold, focusing on her breath, tuning out the city's endless beat. A movement flashes. Celeste Blackwell, hair tied back, face showing equal fear and strength, holds a phone.

"She has it already?" Celeste's voice is low, barely louder than cars passing by. "No—it's not just Lucien. There's another player. I'll get the rest. You do your part when I say."

Her words drift like moths in the damp air. Mariel records, her finger ready. Her heart skips. The shadows behind Celeste grow darker, moving—a group of three men, faces hidden under hoods. Their steps are careful, their size obvious.

The alley narrows. Mariel presses herself against the cold bricks, shaking. She knows how to read danger—square shoulders, quiet steps, a gloved hand even though it's warm. The lead man walks with a limp and a silver ring catching the light.

"Did you hear that?" A low, rough voice breaks the silence.

Every dangerous story starts like this. Every time she has to be quick and quiet to stay lucky. She looks back at the rusty fire escape. Someone shouts. She runs, adrenaline burning, bile rising in her throat.

Gloved fingers brush her coat, but she breaks free, climbing up the metal rungs two at a time, the cold biting her hands.

Boots pound below. She swings across to the next ledge, balance kept by panic and practice, her breath rasping, clouds in the wet air. Behind her, angry curses mix with rain.

She drops into a crowd of night owls, neon glowing, laughter trailing. She slips into a diner—the bell rings, and the warm smell of burnt coffee surrounds her. She leans against a cracked booth, every nerve alert, her skin prickling with fear and purpose.

She dials, her hands shaking, feeding coins into an old payphone that creaks.

"Lucien. I need—" Her voice is rough. "I got caught. Chinatown—Celeste was there. It's bad. I need backup, or a miracle."

Lucien's voice is calm but tense, cutting through the crackle. "Don't go home. I'm sending someone. Meet them by the Bridgeport Line in twenty minutes. Listen to me, Mariel—if you want to stay safe, do what I say." His words feel fragile. She almost laughs.

"After all I've found—after all I know—you really want me to trust you? You're why the city's bleeding out, Lucien."

There's a long pause, rain and breath moving on the line. "Tonight, I'm your only help. Don't make me regret this."

She hangs up, tensing her shoulders, her throat sore. In the diner glass behind her, the world blinks—a threat moving close like a second skin. She steps outside beneath buzzing neon, the city's heavy sky full of hope and danger. Rain falls down her cheeks as she looks past the skyline, thinking of promises, betrayals, and stories still waiting to be t old.

A delivery bike rushes past, splashing water on her boots. She stands alone, wet but unafraid, refusing to give in to fear or painful memories.

She straightens her shoulders, her eyes burning with quiet fire, and promises—soft but sharp—not to stop. The truth is hungry. So is she.

Elsewhere, in another hospital, a man named Darius Hale leans against cold tiles, his eyes full of loss he can't explain. As thunder shakes the city's veins, fate holds its blade—ready but hidden.

Midnight Reckoning

The penthouse office feels like a different world, glowing with city lights shining through its glass walls, casting blue and green reflections on the dark surfaces. The floors are cold marble, smooth and hard. Lucien Blackwell stands by the windows, holding his encrypted phone, carefully choosing whom to text—Marcus Reed, Ivy Thompson, and the DA's nervous informant. He avoids anyone connected to Celeste, knowing that trust is risky. Tonight, even a small sign of betrayal could ruin their fragile partnership.

Below, the city is alive with noise. Mariel Dawson slips into a hallway where old pipes hum and subway trains rumble. Her breath shows in the cold as she talks into a secure earpiece. "Natalia, don't use your usual phone—take the service route, three minutes. Ivy, update the firewall now. Lauren, the first draft is loaded, locked, and timestamped." Her voice is sharp and quick, while rain reflects off the windows. Mariel's nerves are tense, always alert in this restless city.

Marcus Reed arrives first, silent and watchful in his coat. He checks the room carefully, stopping at the table where Ivy's hidden surveillance gear sits in sleek cases. The air smells faintly of solder and cold machines. He gently touches the cameras and transmitters, ensuring that nothing was tampered with after a security breach the day before. He looks tired, like a man who has seen violence.

The elevator opens. Mariel, full of nervous energy, leads Natalia Voss inside. Natalia looks around the penthouse with a mix of amazement and calculation, holding a worn bag close. In seconds, she switches from excitement to calm, slipping backup memory cards into her sleeve. Her citrus perfume mixes with the metallic smell of the r oom.

The side door opens with a code. Lucien lets Lauren Cassidy in. She moves confidently, carrying a slim briefcase. Her eyes are sharp, but her hands are gentle as she places hard drives and files—secret documents wrapped carefully—on the glass table, next to Mariel's notes and a damaged camera.

They gather together—worn, careful, tense. Ivy enters last, wearing a hood and gloves. She silently scans the room with a small black device in her palm, which blinks as she moves around. The room smells faintly of burnt coffee and threat. Lucien locks the heavy, reinforced door, the click sounding firm and final. Everyone looks at him, their faces glowing with city lights and years of hidden stories.

Lucien moves around the table like a conductor getting ready to lead. "Phones off, radios off. Anyone who followed us here works for someone else." His voice is calm but tense, showing cracks beneath his control. Ivy keeps scanning; Mariel moves, dust shining as she spreads out leaked Brotherhood notes and old bank records. The papers smell of tobacco, sweat, and power—a clear map of betrayals.

Marcus breaks the silence with a deep, rough voice. "The Brotherhood doesn't like leaks. The last guy who tried—his apartment was burned within an hour." He looks Lucien in the eye. "If this goes wrong, no one leaves clean."

Silence falls. Natalia bites her lip, Lauren's pen stops, and Ivy focuses as her scanner's green light nears the end.

Mariel puts down another page, her hand still on the table. "We can't wait. Every delay lets them erase someone else." She looks at Lucien, searching for any doubt.

Ivy's device beeps—a clear digital sound. "Nothing's listening but us," she says, with a small, cautious smile. She removes her gloves and flexes her fingers. "I'll run scans every fifteen minutes. Just in case."

Lucien and Mariel exchange a long, quiet look over the documents. The city's glow reflects in their eyes. This moment is the start of something risky and unchangeable as the night swallows Manhattan's lights.

City lights flicker through the high windows, partly blocked by blinds, making patterns on the shiny floor. Lucien stands at the head of the glass table, his sleeve brushing against a steel briefcase. The air feels heavy with worry, mixed with the smell of rain, electricity, and the hum from Ivy's laptop. Lauren shifts nervously, adjusting her glasses. Natalia, barefoot, stands near the wall holding press badges and secure drives.

Lucien opens the locked case and hands out thin folders and encrypted USB sticks. His hands are tense, revealing his stress. Each file contains secrets about the Brotherhood: money trails, fake charity groups, shady properties—years of hidden crime laid out clearly. He talks about risky targets—clubs where money is laundered, shell companies, offices hidden from light. His eyes stop on Marcus as he names a location in the Bronx with weak muscle on the payroll, then on Ivy as he points to a weak firewall in the Orion Club's satellite office.

Lucien remembers past failures—when one unprotected call led to death and disgrace. Tonight, everything is about fixing those mistakes. His control is strict, based on fear. One loose end could destroy everything.

Mariel signals Natalia. The big wall lights up, showing a timeline with dates, mugshots, and diagrams of money and violence. Mariel explains the plan: the digital wave will hit just as subpoenas arrive, headlines break, and viral news spreads, exposing the Brotherhood's secrets. Her voice sounds tired but sharp, wanting the world to see the fall of Lucien's hidden world, even if it costs them all.

But the plan has weak points. Ivy's list of secret sources may disappear if exposed. Natalia scrolls through backup channels, reminding them that if the main network fails, freelance journalists will keep the story alive.

Marcus leans forward, his scarred hands in the light. "They'll come hard," he warns. "Remember Benson's fate. If it gets dangerous, you leave immediately—no arguments." He names escape spots firmly. "Plan your exit now."

Lauren pushes consent forms across the table, tapping her pen nervously. "If we release these before the AG's office checks them, they'll bury you in lawsuits, and we'll lose the public's attention. I want one official approval, or we delay release by two days." She looks serious, fearing legal attacks.

Ivy types quickly, and a cyber plan appears on the screen: fake signals, automatic news updates, social media distractions to buy time after the first breach. "Once I activate it, their communications will fall into chaos. We get only fifteen minutes before they catch on. After that, we disappear."

Lucien gathers the plans. Each is risky, filled with lessons from his past. The Brotherhood once seemed all-powerful—he recalls meetings with Caius Drake and Silas Carver, dangerous men always watching. Now power feels fragile. Even in this glass room, the city's secrets fight beneath him, reminders of past losses.

He asks for agreement, his voice urgent. "This is the last time we speak openly. After tonight, no calls, no texts, nothing that can be traced. Commit or leave."

Mariel nods firmly, sorting her notes. "We need new backup channels. Ivy, handle backup servers. Natalia, list press contacts Lauren wouldn't know. Every leak is a risk, but we save every story, file, name."

Natalia agrees softly. Burner phones are passed around. The team waits, tense, memorizing details and meeting spots. Outside, the wind shakes the glass. Each member brings their strength—Natalia's calm, Marcus's toughness, Lauren's focus, Ivy's drive. Far away, others like Darius Hale, Orion Vega, and Silas Carver play their parts in this dangerous game. Here, trust is almost as important as the evidence t hey hold.

One by one, plans are set. Lucien collects all drives and locks them away. Ivy erases traces from the network, wiping passwords silently.

Mariel touches Natalia's wrist lightly, speaking low but clearly: "There's no turning back. Once we do this, we burn our bridges." The city's lights shimmer in her serious eyes.

Natalia nods quietly, her jaw trembling slightly. The storm outside grows. The team waits, ready for either disaster or the truth.

Lucien stays in the open doorway as the others walk away, the penthouse growing quiet as if the world is holding its breath. Purple city lights fade through the blinds. Mariel stands near the low-lit bar, moving quickly and skillfully—stacking papers, putting away the camera, setting her worn notebook on top. Lucien approaches softly, the sound of his shoes almost silent on the carpet. His cufflink shines in the dim light. When his hand brushes her wrist—a light, careful touch—she feels alert but doesn't pull away. She looks up, and the moment stretches, full of unspoken things.

Outside, Manhattan sparkles and moves. Sirens echo off glass towers. The city's night noises—horns, cab doors slamming, wet sidewalks—fill the air. Shadows move against the tall windows, creating a quiet space in the storm. Mariel breathes softly on the glass as she opens the door to a private lounge. Inside feels quiet, like a safe bubble. Lucien follows, closing the door softly behind them, as if locking a saf e.

Inside, the air smells of fine brandy, old wood, and faint cigarette smoke. The city's restless glow colors Lucien's profile blue and silver. He waits behind Mariel, close but not touching, filling the room with his presence.

Mariel puts her hand on the granite bar, steadying herself, listening to her heartbeat among the city noise. Then she says, "This is bigger than any story I've chased. Trusting you could ruin me." Her voice is low, mixed with fear and certainty. "Or you. Maybe both."

The room holds its breath. Lucien reads her words quietly, then sits on the edge of a leather couch. He keeps his usual calm pose, but his hand on his knee is tense. His eyes, deep and restless, reflect the city lights as he looks at her. In the silence, he weighs the truth and the words left unsaid.

"I know you may never fully trust me," he says softly, "but what we have has never been a secret to me. I don't know if that's my strength or my weakness."

He leans back, shoulders tight, a faint scar shadowing his jaw shows his alertness. Mariel presses her thumb hard on the bar. The city outside keeps moving, but inside, time slows.

She turns toward him with eyes full of conflict. "You scare me," she admits honestly. "Not because of what you've done or who you protect. It's what happens when I'm near you. I want the truth, Lucien. I want to believe I'm still the woman I was. But every time you look at me, I lose my balance. I don't know if I can trust you and still trust myself."

He doesn't try to close the space between them. Instead, his voice lowers, losing some control. "I see you, Mariel. Even at your toughest, even when you want to tear down everything I stand for." His voice breaks slightly. "What I want, what you make me feel, breaks my plans every time. Maybe that's what scares you. That it's not just me."

Another city might grow quiet at midnight, but New York never stops. In the penthouse, Mariel's pulse races. She remembers betrayals—friends, mentors, her own desire for something pure in a dark world. How many times has she weighed her beliefs against her feelings? How often has she wanted justice, only to be pulled toward uncertainty? Working with Lucien is a careful risk. Letting him in is even more dangerous.

In this stolen moment, their partnership is fragile—a new thing that could break easily. Every touch, every word shows how hard trust is. She wants to come closer, to believe she can trust him. But the words get stuck.

A sharp electronic beep breaks the silence—a security alert from Ivy's backup system. Lucien jumps up, reaching for his phone. Mariel's heart races, fear pushing out old doubts. They look at each other across the shiny floor—regret, warning, and hope in their eyes.

Neither says a word as they head to the door. Lucien places his hand on the glass, pausing before opening it. Mariel waits a moment longer. Their eyes meet, the tension between them as electric as the city outside, full of fear, hope, and all the things they haven't dared to s ay.

They step into the hallway, fate close behind, footsteps echoing toward danger. Their partnership—and something darker—holds them together.

Shadows Clash

The Orion Club is almost silent this late, its earlier noise replaced by the quiet hum of air vents and the soft steps of Lucien Blackwell's Italian leather shoes on shiny floors. He slips through a secret side door known only to trusted members. Past flickering security screens casting a blue light over empty lounges, he moves into a dim hallway where shadows gather like soft velvet. He nods to a silent guard by an unmarked door—there but not really seen, faces blank. The air smells of old smoke, expensive drinks, and something sharp and metallic beneath the surface.

Lucien's hand brushes the heavy curtain, catching briefly on a seam—revealing his tension. He steps inside. The private lounge is dark, lit by a deep amber glow. Black marble reflects faint light in broken pieces, showing a lone figure sitting under the faint eye of a security camera.

Elias Kane, as always, holds a power that draws attention even when people want to look away. Sitting in a tall leather chair, he remains still, only his jaw moving slightly. His eyes meet Lucien's—steady and unreadable. His long fingers tap slowly on the armrest. On a small table to his side: untouched whiskey and a thin folder wrapped in worn black leather.

Lucien crosses to the chair across from him, moving carefully and with control. He sits on the cool leather, and for a moment, both men just breathe. The air feels heavy, thick with smoke and old stories—of men like Caius Drake or Silas Carver, names known in the city's underworld. Somewhere inside the club, rumors of new troubles—Orion Vega's latest scandal, Darius Hale's cold actions—float around, distant but always present.

"Stop the act," Lucien says, his voice low and sharp. "I want answers. Money is missing from Kane's records, secret offshore accounts opened with names that hide their true owners—you. And people are disappearing. Informants, Brotherhood members, even that courier—you know the one—two nights ago. Where are they?"

Elias narrows his eyes, lips tight and unreadable. He lifts his hand, fingers tapping slowly on the black marble. After a pause, he speaks quietly, without emotion: "This city is a war zone, Lucien. The Brotherhood stays strong because it is ruthless where others hesitate. Bribes keep the city officials looking away. Those who don't obey—the contractors?—they have accidents. Sad but necessary. Rivals learn quickly their limits."

He lets the words hang in the smoky air. "We do what it takes to keep power. The city looks clean not because everyone is innocent, but because we make sure no blood stays where it can't be cleaned."

Lucien's hands curl into fists, pale knuckles pressing into his trousers. He looks around the room, breathes in the faint smell of whiskey, and feels a deep fracture growing inside him. His jaw tightens. "You're not answering me. Where are the bodies, Elias? Davison, Petras, Fenn?"

Elias shows a flash of anger—a warning. "Be careful," he says softly, his voice icy. "You know better than anyone how we handle things. You approved moves—silencing voices. Don't develop a conscience now because the taste has changed."

Lucien's glare grows sharper. "There's a difference between protecting the Brotherhood and destroying what little honor we have left. These weren't threats. They were warnings, then killings."

Elias leans forward, his voice like a blade. "You sat with me at those meetings, Lucien. Don't forget your place. Loyalty is what keeps a man alive here. If you ask questions that echo in the wrong places, you become an echo yourself. Remember those who forgot their loyalties."

"You're threatening me," Lucien says quietly, his eyes steady.

"I'm reminding you." Elias stands, his shadow long as the camera light flickers above. "The Orion Brotherhood lives because it never hesitates. Not out of fear, love, or for you."

Lucien's surprise is clear—rare and stark. Elias moves toward the side door, footsteps silent. The door closes with a click. Shadows fill the space where power, and the man who holds it, just disappeared.

Mariel's morning begins in dim light, city sounds muffled by thick curtains and the quiet purr of her cat by the window. She blinks away sleep and reaches for her phone, her thumb hovering over the locked app—a habit born of fear and need. There's a message left overnight. Plain words:

Stop digging or your story becomes your obituary.

Her eyes stay on the screen, her heartbeat quickening. The room feels smaller, shadows reaching across the floor. The familiar smell of old coffee and city dust surrounds her, a mix of comfort and threat. She deletes the message, sets the phone down quietly, and wonders which neighbor might be watching. Outside, the city moves on—unbothered as always.

At the Herald, the newsroom buzzes with a fake calm. Mariel's desk still smells like last night's takeout. Editors rush by, voices sharp with deadline stress. She swallows her fear and heads for Lauren Cassidy's glass office. The glass shows parts of her face—determined but doubtful.

Inside, Lauren sits upright, her suit neat, her eyes hard to read. Two senior editors sit with her, ready to take notes. Lauren gestures for Mariel to sit, her tone firm but gentle.

"Mariel, sit down. We need to talk—off the record."

"I guessed," Mariel says, pulling her coat tighter. "Is this about the Kane records?"

Lauren taps the table. "Your latest story is explosive. But you don't name sources. No proof shown. This isn't just risky for you. It's a disaster waiting to happen for the Herald."

"We built our name on taking risks," Mariel says sharply. "Or has that changed since the Orion Club started controlling the city's money?"

An older editor leans in: "If these claims are wrong, lawsuits will bury us."

Lauren's eyes narrow. "We all want justice. But rumors could destroy the paper. Have you thought about the rest of us?"

Her words cut deeper than Mariel expected. For a moment, her confidence shakes under Lauren's careful concern. She thinks of Caius Drake's cold poker face and Seraphina Hayes's words about the pressure of power—a reminder that even the strongest can fall under shadows.

She exhales slowly. "I won't back down. I know what I found."

Lauren's lips tighten, her eyes showing tired acceptance. "Then bring me the names, the documents, the proof. Our protection isn't as strong as you think."

The silence holds tension. When Mariel stands, her hands are white with grip. Around the newsroom, some nod quietly, while others avoid looking, afraid. Trust is rare here. Today, she has none.

Outside in Midtown, the city feels different—oily, sharp, alive with secrets. A subway screech shakes her bones as she slips into a wet alleyway. The address from her tip fits: a clean, glass office that feels empty, like the kind Darius Hale's company might own before fading into shell companies and fake accounts.

She waits, pressed to the cold bricks, her fingers numb. Boots click—a courier, face hidden under a hat, leaves the building, blending into the crowd. Mariel stays. Her skin tingles. A car's headlights shine at the alley's end—a black sedan speeds in, engine growling. She throws herself behind a smelly dumpster, its cold metal pressing into her hands. Tires screech on wet pavement. The car's dark windows catch the fading light and, for a moment, reflect her tense face.

Adrenaline tastes metallic as the car speeds away. She counts her breaths, her cheeks stinging from gravel. Trust no one—that old lesson from Lila Moreno after a hospital stabbing: the world is full of hands that heal and hands that hurt, and they often look the same at first.

Back at the Herald, the air is colder, thick with suspicion. Mariel's hands shake as she calls Natalia, fumbling. They meet in a rainy café smelling of stale espresso and wet wool. Natalia orders coffee, slides it over, and squeezes Mariel's wrist, steadying her. Outside, neon lights shimmer on puddles, and quiet city noise presses in.

"I got a threat this morning," Mariel whispers. "Almost got hit by a car today. The paper's tense—I think they're watching us. I can't tell if it's fear for me or just fear."

"You need to be less visible," Natalia says calmly. "Run stories in teams. Change where you go. Never go straight home. If you think you're followed, don't be a hero. I'll check those shell accounts for you—there are links between Kane and Vega's old tech businesses. Hidden but there."

Mariel's shoulders shake, but her jaw stays firm. "I can't stop now," she says.

"I know," Natalia replies softly but firmly. "But you have to stay alive to make a difference. If something feels wrong, call me first."

They part under dark clouds, night settling on wet streets and distant traffic. Mariel doesn't look back, standing in the gray city evening, fear and determination tangled together. She takes a deep breath and steps into the dark, more determined—and more alone—than ever.

Lightning cuts through the rainy sky as Lucien Blackwell unlocks his penthouse door. Rain shines on his coat. The city below spreads out, restless, lights flickering with water on the windows. He takes off his coat and throws it on a quiet velvet chair. The silence inside feels strange, heavy with echoes from the Orion Club. His footsteps ring sharply on the polished floor.

He goes to the liquor cart and pours whiskey into a glass. The burn is quick, a warm relief, but it does nothing to cool the chill crawling on his skin or ease the memory of Elias Kane's threat. Lucien's hand stays on the glass, his thumb tracing the edge. He looks out at the city, lights blending like watercolors—bright, harsh, uncaring.

If he left now—ignored Kane's words, played the fixer—would he sleep? He doubts it. Faces of those who vanished on Brotherhood orders press behind his eyes: an informant crying, clutching a train ticket; a young man whose last call Lucien ended with a signature; each memory burning.

He crosses the room and opens an encrypted case on his desk. The soft click of locks opening—a code as familiar as breathing. Files spread across the desk—emails, accounts, records written in cold, -official language. The air smells dry with old paper and caution. One folder marked with a red slash holds details of the informant's death. Elias's signature loops on the edges—almost careless.

Lucien's jaw tightens. Some names connect to his own choices. There is no pride left in the precise work that once defined him. The club's empire, so orderly from the outside, is rotten inside—bribes hidden in numbers, justice bought and sold. Power always costs something.

He scrolls through messages on his laptop, the low sound blending with the storm outside. Every secret message between Brotherhood members deepens the crack inside him: officials forced down with threats, city leaders paid off to stay quiet. A plan to blame a rival gang for three deaths shows clearly. The facts pile up, heavy and cold. He reads until the words blur and become white noise.

Outside, the city moves through its own storms—waitresses hustling, sleepless billionaires, surgeons haunted by their work, tech leaders surrounded by ghosts of progress, powerful men so far away they seem like myths. He sees glimpses: Caius Drake, stern as he leaves a fancy dinner; Seraphina Hayes, umbrella crooked, phone to her ear entering a bright café. A few floors down, Silas Carver's office keeps one lamp burning. Past the river, Darius Hale's lights are off, except for a hospital screen's blue glow; a nurse—Lila, he thinks—stands by him, bright against fatigue.

Lucien's phone lights up on the desk, showing a half-written message to Mariel. His finger freezes above the screen, held back by doubt—a blank to fill, a line he can't decide to cross. He imagines her, bent over messy notes, jaw firm, eyes fierce with hope. She deserves neither silence nor danger from him. What if warning her only makes Kane move against her? What if leaving now is the only way to keep her safe? This choice eats at his resolve: protect Mariel or betray everything he once stood for with the Brotherhood. Hope changes into guilt.

Every direction leads to futures he can't trust. If he quietly gathers proof, can he beat Kane's power—his reach, his ability to sense disloyalty before words? What will it cost to break free from the Brotherhood's dark control? If he falls, who pays first? Tonight's storm is no accident. The whole city shakes with questions left unanswered.

He closes the case. Sets down the empty glass with care. Moves to the window, palms cold against the glass, watching cars weave through shiny streets. Sirens scream and fade. Another world waits—a city full of haunted men, desperate lovers, mortals who dare to betray gods. The skyline is like a circuit board, each light a secret signal. He wonders if one belongs to Mariel. He wonders if tomorrow he'll find the strength to be her shield—or if saving her means breaking every rule he once lived by.

His dark shape stands against the city's pulse. Determined and unsure, hard as smoke. For now, Lucien stands, rain on the glass and the city's night echoing in his blood, promising he won't go back to the dark easily—or without a fight.

The Breaking Point

Lucien walks into the quiet Orion Club, the doors closing softly behind him, blocking out the noise of the city. Dim light shines from wall lamps, touching the dark velvet curtains and casting shadows on the thick carpets and polished wood. The air is heavy with the smell of tobacco, old whiskey, and expensive cologne. He fits in perfectly: wearing a sharp gray suit, his shoes silent on the marble floor, moving smoothly like a blade cutting through silk. Around him, men and women in fancy clothes talk quietly at tables and lean on shadowy bars while a piano plays a sad tune. They look at him with the respect he expects.

But near the tall windows, someone breaks the pattern. Mariel Dawson stands there, a spark of fire in the dark room. Her dark hair is pulled back, her shoulders straight, and a bright teal shirt shows just under her plain jacket. She holds a worn leather folder tightly. Her presence is as shocking as the folder. The doormen stare at her longer than usual. One checks his radio and gives Lucien a silent signal: not yet. Let Lucien go first.

Lucien walks toward her, each step quiet but full of meaning. The club seems to change: Marcus Reed stands with his arms crossed, jaw tense; Caius Drake watches from the dark bar, his face unreadable; some minor members move closer, pretending to talk. At the main table, Elias Kane sits with tight lips and white knuckles on his glass of scotch. Lucien feels power tightening, getting ready.

Mariel speaks sharply, breaking the silence. "So this is where you hide—behind velvet curtains and glass, while the city suffers lies." She raises the folder, her knuckles white, and faces Lucien directly. "Let everyone see it. Blackwell, you made fake evidence. You destroyed lives to keep this place safe. I have proof."

Lucien feels a rush—shame, anger, but also fear and pride—seeing her stand strong in the middle of this dangerous place. The Brotherhood's eyes sting him, full of judgment and curiosity. His usual calm breaks. He speaks quietly, trying to control his voice but with anger inside. "You think this place is run on stories and honor? Take that folder outside, Mariel, and face the truth. It costs lives."

She laughs bitterly. "I know enough. Secrets like yours kill innocence. How many more will you sacrifice to stay safe, Lucien? Or are you just protecting your pride?"

The room grows colder. Lucien sees the Brotherhood split and shift, alliances changing. Marcus's hand tightens on his glass. Elias watches them both, trying to read loyalty and danger. Lucien wants to stop her, protect her, shake her—his feelings are torn. "If you show what's in that folder," he says tightly, "you'll start a war you can't fight. You'll risk yourself, the innocent, the city. I won't let you."

"How noble," Mariel replies, eyes bright but hurt. "If you want to keep me safe, then stop playing God with people's lives."

Elias looks cold and sharp at Lucien. The balance settles. Lucien feels the moment could destroy everything or change it forever. The silence grows—each heartbeat loud. He steps closer to Mariel, putting himself between her and the Brotherhood's guards.

"You don't understand what you're up against," he says quietly, his voice breaking a bit. "You don't have to do this."

Mariel dares him. "I don't have to. But I will." She pushes the folder into his chest. "I'm done with your game. I'll bring it all down if I must."

Their hands touch briefly—cold and electric, full of memories and risks. Anything could break: her, him, the fragile power holding this empire together. The room holds its breath.

She turns and walks away, her dark coat flowing like midnight velvet, moving through the heavy oak doors. Neon light brushes her figure. Those left behind watch Lucien as if waiting for an explosion. At the main table, Elias's stare is icy and fierce—warning of trouble beyond tonight.

Afterward, a glass breaks. Lucien stands still, the folder pressed to his chest, the future opening wide beneath him.

The city looks like an open wound, neon lights pulsing beneath the dark night. On a rooftop five stories up, Mariel Dawson breathes in the cold air, which disappears as fast as the courage bringing her there. The chill cuts through her coat, biting her cheeks and ears. She hugs herself tightly, pressing her fists to her chest, staring at the chaos below—Manhattan alive and restless, unaware of the secrets breaking open inside it.

The night is full of noise and color. Honking cars mix with distant sirens. Smells—grease from food stands, burning tobacco, cold rain—float upward. She tastes adrenaline—sharp and bitter—and feels her own defiance thumping in her head.

Car lights shine like rivers of white and gold across the streets, but up here there's just Mariel, the wind, and her fast thoughts. Her jaw tightens; every muscle feels tense and raw from the earlier fight. Her phone glows faintly in her hand, the screen black like the sky. She turns it, feeling its edge dig into her palm. She feels taller and more exposed at once.

Faces from the club flash through her mind—shock, anger, mocking smiles—but it's Lucien's look she can't forget. The hurt behind his careful eyes, hidden beneath calm, stays under her skin. Did she see fear there? For her? Or for himself?

The wind rattles small stones by her boots. She shivers, holding back a scream. Is revenge worth this loneliness?

The rooftop is her refuge, but it's colder than she thought. She breathes deep, filling her lungs with the city's chill, and remembers the past—moments broken and shaky like her nerves. Lucien's hand on her back in a small apartment lit by candlelight, the rare smile when she made him laugh. His low voice sharing secrets late at night. The slow touch of his thumb on her wrist, like a question they never answered.

Those moments crash now—drowned by shouting, betrayal under the club's dim lights. Her body remembers his touch and fury. The danger tasted addictive and destructive. She misses what was, even as her mind pulls away.

A future with Lucien seems impossible, but being swallowed by his secrets is worse. She watches the street, feeling truth hiding just under the headlights and endless ambition. She wonders—if she goes through with this, will he survive what comes? Will she?

Regret bites hollow inside her. She wants to yell at him, say she's sorry and angry and scared all at once. She wants to ask why he makes it so hard to hate him. If she hadn't chased his truth, maybe her own would be safer.

Is justice possible when your heart fights your belief?

Sometimes she thinks of Caius Drake, ruthless in loud speakeasies, tough and unbreakable—a hero from Book 1 who left feelings behind for power. Then Silas Carver, always planning in the shadows, using silence as a weapon, or Darius Hale, a surgeon from Book 3, living on the edge between helping and hurting. Mariel's city makes heroes and destroys them. She wonders what mark she will leave in this neon s torm.

Below, a cab drives by, its radio playing soft, sad music. Mariel wishes she could be anonymous: a woman with nothing to lose and no secrets burning inside. Instead, her life hangs by a thread. If she reveals the story, fire will fall on her and Lucien. If she hides it, guilt will never le ave.

Far away, Lucien sits in an office lit by cold light, his tie loose, breath misting on his clenched fists. The room smells of ink and fine leather, moonlight cutting through glass. He holds the folder she gave him, papers slipping. Guilt shakes him—old and quiet, born from choices made in courtrooms and Brotherhood halls. Sometimes he imagines a life without duty, with a woman who laughs and forgives. That life is always just out of reach.

On the rooftop, Mariel unlocks her phone and types: "Ready to move forward. High risk. Need backup." The name Ivy is at the top of the screen—a small light in the storm. Her thumb shakes, then presses send.

The wind picks up. The city waits for her next move. In the office of steel and shadows, Lucien opens the folder, secrets spilling under harsh light, and finally lets the weight sit on him.

Manhattan's cold, endless lights shine beyond the steel and glass of Lucien Blackwell's office. A strip of city starlight runs along his glass decanter, reflecting on his dark desk. Brothers gather quietly: Marcus Reed stands close to the shelves, alert with eyes narrowed, arms folded to block out the city's bright threat. Two men in dark suits and secret loyalties stand by the heavy doors, quiet and watchful.

Lucien's tie is loose. His heart beats fast under his perfect shirt. The mixed smells of leather and ink fill the room, mingled with a sharp feeling of fear and resolve hanging in the air. He doesn't sit. Tonight, standing feels safer.

"I'm not asking for blood," Lucien says quietly, his voice calm but sharp, like a lawyer ready to fight. "No one will touch Mariel. Even if Elias tells you." His words fall heavily.

A pause. One brother shifts. Marcus's mouth turns, half doubt, half slow agreement. "What if she moves first? What if she shines the city's light on us? Even you can't hide then."

Lucien meets Marcus's look, his eyes flickering between coldness and conscience. "We stay ahead. We control the story, or we all fall, including her." His words feel colder than he wants.

The men murmur, losing confidence against a leader who faces ruin without fear. Somewhere else, Caius Drake talks business nearby, and Silas Carver moves silently in glass halls. Lucien wonders if all city kings share the same hunger and fear.

He explains the plan in short, clear points: control the story, use power over rival groups, pressure judges and officials—the tools of survival turning even as everything threatens to fall apart. He makes no move against Mariel Dawson; her name pulses through the quiet like a fuse.

Marcus looks at him, quieter now. "Elias knows you won't do what's needed. He's already acting. This plan might buy us time." He lowers his head. "But it might kill you. Or her."

Lucien feels a chill down his spine. The Brotherhood's secrets bind him like chains. For a moment, guilt almost breaks his face: Is this hunger for control and redemption worth the city's ruin? He tightens his jaw. He's trapped by his own code, hoping for forgiveness from a woman who could ruin him.

He sends them away; Marcus stays a bit then leaves, footsteps softer than his threat. Lucien stands alone. The room feels huge, the city's pulse beating with memories of better times.

Far below, another story unfolds in a small apartment.

Mariel's place is warm late at night. Soft light glows on gray and teal walls—a quiet heart in the stormy city. Her laptop glows blue on her sharp face and shaky hands. She walks barefoot on the cool wood floor, breathing fast from nerves she won't name.

Natalia Voss sits on the couch, wrapped in a plaid blanket, concern clear in her brown eyes. The two of them show worry and duty: Mariel's hands shine with adrenaline as she opens locked files and listens to voicemails, each broken voice another nail in the Brotherhood's coffin.

Natalia speaks softly. "Mari, this is… all of it. But if you go through with this, are you ready for what happens next?"

"I have to be." Mariel's voice shakes but is firm. She opens one last folder. "I never wanted a different ending."

"Do you really mean it?" Natalia asks, protective but scared. "Even if it ruins every chance with him? You can't hesitate, Mari. You can't 'sort of' burn the world down."

"I know." Mariel looks steady. "If I lose him, if the city turns on me, I still have to do this. I can't give in. Not for love. Not for anyone."

Natalia squeezes her hand. "Then I'll help you. But I wish you'd let me worry for you, just this once."

A phone vibrates—on Lucien's desk and in Mariel's hand at the same time, as if fate wants one last connection. The city's distant sirens and wind fall silent as they each answer. His voice is soft and broken; hers, quiet and brave.

"Mariel—"

"Lucien—"

A pause. Words half-said—sorry, promises, warnings—hang between them. The divide is wide, fragile as thin glass.

"It's moving too fast," Lucien says, his voice breaking. "We don't have time."

"I know. I think this is it, right?"

"Whatever happens next, we can't take it back."

"We can't." Her voice shakes as city lights flicker on her pale face. "But I won't run. I won't let them silence me."

A long silence. Then the call ends, the city swallowing their last words.

Lucien looks at the skyline, his heart heavy. Across the dark, Mariel does the same. Somewhere, a hospital window glows—inside, a surgeon named Darius Hale works on midnight patients, his world trembling toward its own storm. The future hangs on a knife's edge, all fates linked in the neon night.

Echoes Before Dawn

The first touch of dawn slips through the glass walls, lighting the penthouse in silver and washed-out gold. Lucien steps in, silent except for the soft whisper of his shoes over stone. He stops on the threshold, the city pressed against the glass behind Mariel's silhouette—a dark figure shaped by the slow promise of morning. Manhattan unspools below, towers catching the pale bloom of sunlight, fractured by shadows that seem reluctant to loosen their hold.

Mariel stands at the edge, arms crossed tightly, her reflection ghostly on the pane. The air is brittle, every sound suspended as if waiting for some verdict. The scent of strong coffee lingers, unfinished on the kitchen counter behind him, underscoring the hour's loneliness. Lucien watches her shoulders rise and fall. He owes her words, but every syllable feels dangerous.

She turns, the city's glow catching the line of her jaw. Her eyes meet his, unwavering, daring him to fill the silence.

"You think one apology erases everything?" Mariel's voice is low and sharp. "You built your world on secrets, and now you want mine."

Lucien swallows. The weight of all he's hidden presses against his chest—the shell companies, the backroom deals, the double life carved out of lies. Regret sours at the back of his throat. Yet habit tugs at him: don't surrender ground, don't reveal more than planned.

"That's not what I want," he murmurs, his voice steady out of necessity, though the restraint costs him. "I want you to know everything that matters now. The lines I drew—they kept you safe, or I tried to believe they did."

She lets out a breath, her shoulders stiffening, and steps away from the glass. "Safe? Or silent?"

Their words slice through the quiet, but there's a deeper current—hurt tangled with longing, trust gouged and raw. Mariel watches him, the wounded fire in her gaze an accusation and an invitation both.

"I lied. I thought protecting you meant keeping you in the dark," Lucien admits, forcing each word past the instinct to lock them down. "But I kept too much. That's not defense; it's betrayal, and I know it."

A muscle in Mariel's cheek tightens. She's close enough now that he can see the smudge of fatigue under her eyes, the stubborn set of her jaw.

"Betrayal isn't the half of it." Her voice wavers, softening just enough for him to hear the devastation beneath.

He takes a step closer, gentling his approach as if she's made of glass. Lucien raises his hand slowly, waiting for her to flinch. When she doesn't, he brushes his knuckles against her cheek. Mariel's breath hitches; her eyes flutter half-shut. In that space—compressed between dawn and confession—the two of them exist miles from the city's noise.

His hand lingers. Their breaths become shallow, tangled, warming the space between them. Lucien's pulse is thunderous in his ears, his fear a live wire beneath his skin—fear that she'll turn away, or worse: forgive him too easily.

"Don't," she says softly. But she doesn't move. He feels her searching him for sincerity, for something that won't break if she leans in.

They make their way to the wide window seat, cushions yielding beneath them. The city sprawls below, but up here is hush and light. Lucien keeps his hands folded until Mariel's fingers, tentative, brush against his. He's the one who trembles.

"I want to trust you," she says after a long silence. "But you're good at making people believe things, Lucien. Especially me."

He doesn't look away. He tucks a stray curl behind her ear, his touch stripped of the usual calculation. "I'm tired of pretending. Whatever happens, you get all of me. Not the fixer. Not the lawyer. Only what's left."

Her thumb finds the scar at his jaw—he has never let anyone linger there before. Their faces are close enough for Lucien to taste the faint bitterness of her last sip of coffee, to catch the trace of almond from her shampoo.

"And if it all falls apart?"

"Then we fall together," he answers, the words leaving him bare.

A flicker of something fierce and bright enters Mariel's gaze. "Don't make promises you can't keep."

"I promise. You have my trust—no shadows this time. You want the truth; it's yours."

She tightens her grip. "And I swear I won't run. Even if it destroys us."

Outside, sirens sigh in the distance, another day roaring to life below. Sunlight leaps across the glass, illuminating them in warmth as if the city itself were blessing this fragile peace.

Lucien pulls Mariel into his embrace, her head resting against his heart. No more secrets. Just skin, heartbeat, hope—and the slow birth of a new alliance, golden and trembling in the new day's first light.

Mid-morning light slices through the glass walls of Lucien Blackwell's office, Manhattan stretching in mirrored fragments far below. Blueprints, manila folders, and a scattering of burner phones clutter the enormous conference table—transmuting its usual order into a war room's chaos. The scent of fresh ink, old coffee, and chilled steel fills the air, mixing with the distant rumble of city traffic below. Papers rustle under Mariel's hand as she fans out her notes, every gesture brisk and precise, her jaw set with resolve.

Lucien shrugs off his jacket and drapes it over a chair, watching her. Her fingers dance across colored paper tabs: transfers, offshore routes, shell companies. She doesn't glance up. Her focus is scalpel-sharp.

"These are the dummy corporations," she says. "Six in the Caymans, three in Switzerland, God knows how many in Delaware. Money moves every forty-eight hours. IWY Capital pretends it's investment income, but nothing substantial ever lands in any account on record."

He nods, his lips pressed in a thin line. "The accounts are fronted by layers—traders, real estate, even charities. Complex enough to repel most auditors. But all it takes is one persistent journalist..." His gaze lingers, a flicker of admiration beneath practiced indifference.

Her smile is tight. "One persistent fixer, too. What are you hiding for them, Lucien?"

He picks up a thick folder and flips it open, splaying confidential legal briefs across the table. "Pre-emptive injunctions. Quiet settlements. Bribed board members, threatened IRS agents. There's more—statutes bent until they're almost unrecognizable. The Brotherhood isn't just laundering money. They're swallowing the legal system whole." He spreads the papers. His hands betray no tremor, but every motion speaks of tension wound tight as wire.

She meets his gaze, chin raised. "So what do we do—blow it all up in the press and hope no one gets shot before lunch, or crawl so slowly they have time to erase us?"

His laugh is dry. "You want slow when time's a blade at your neck?"

"Rushed is how mistakes happen."

He leans in, his voice low. "Mistakes happen when you underestimate the enemy. Elias Kane has contacts in every precinct, judges on speed dial. This isn't a single thread to pull—it's a web choking the city." His finger taps the site of a coded phone number scrawled in his precise script. "We strike now, and hard. But the exit has to be planned, or someone—"

"—dies screaming in a side alley?" Mariel's eyes flash—a challenge and plea mingled in their depths. Her reflection in the window behind him is ghosted by dawn's last gold. "Fine. We strike, but keep every door open."

"You trust me to keep you safe?" His voice is edged, vulnerability hidden in a sliver of dark humor.

She hesitates, only a heartbeat, before nodding. "I trust that you want the truth out. That's enough."

He nods, drawing oxygen deep into his lungs, savoring its bite. This woman is as relentless as the city devouring them both.

He watches her draft encrypted instructions, her thumbs hitting keys in a furious rhythm. Code words, rendezvous points, backup plans. Every message is a wager of loyalty—a signal fire for allies scattered across the boroughs. Lucien, meanwhile, thumbs through burner contacts: Caius Drake, known for surgical precision in financial warfare, ghosts his number with a single cryptic message—a ripple set loose in the investment empire's glass towers. He glances at a folder,

Darius Hale's name scrawled in the margin; the surgeon's moral clarity and cold detachment might soon prove just as useful as a blade at midnight. Even Orion Vega, scandal-loving genius, and Silas Carver, the unfathomable tactician, flit as shadows at the circuit's edge—reminders that the Brotherhood's reach is hydra-headed.

Lucien scrawls backup plans on the whiteboard: meet points, legal smokescreens, coded signals for when even the strongest doors can't hold. Mariel paces, phone pressed to her ear, lines of tension at the corner of her mouth flexing as she checks with Natalia on the press grid and Ivy on network penetration. The hum of vigilance is everywhere—a soft buzz from Ivy's cyberwarfare protocols running in the background; Natalia's steady, accented reassurance filtered through static.

A silence settles as the final pieces click into place.

She circles back to the table. "Everyone's ready. Your insiders—are you sure they'll hold?"

He nods, his gaze steady. "If they don't, no one leaves this office alive anyway. I've covered every angle. Except—" He looks at her, and for a fleeting second, lets hope tremble on the edges. "Except whether you'll still be here if it all crashes down."

She slides her fingers over his, a brief, electric touch. "Ask me when the city's different."

His smile—crooked, real—flares and then fades as he wipes the board clean, erasing the final uncertain mark. Across the paper-littered battlefield, their eyes lock. Their pact is formed—not just of strategy, but of the fraught, fragile trust that survives everything except surrender.

The brownstone sits quietly in the fading afternoon, a hunchbacked silhouette stitched into the city's tumult. Natalia's sneakers make barely a sound on the stoop, Ivy at her heels, hands full with a battered messenger bag and a box of gear. Ivy's breath fogs a faint circle on the glass as she glances up, nerves making her fidget with the magnetized chip in her palm. The keypad flashes, brief and clinical—her silent greeting. Something about the quiet here feels deeper than usual, darker, as if the building itself is holding its breath.

Inside, Marcus Reed's bulk fills the narrow hall, the Brotherhood's shield sewn into his jacket like an afterthought. The scent is all concrete and metal, the low hum of distant pipes in place of welcome. He scans their faces—Natalia's determined, Ivy's edgy, the unnamed Brotherhood insider unreadable at his side. A nod passes between Marcus and Ivy, loaded and wary.

Lucien waits at the head of the makeshift table in the center room, glass shards of dusk slicing in through grime-dulled windows. Mariel stands just under the lone bulb, her shadow stretching long behind her, a folder pressed to her chest. The table's surface is a battlefield: blueprints scrawled over in graphite, burner phones, tangled wires, packets of evidence. On the edge, a single disposable coffee cup emits a bitter aroma, caffeine clinging to desperation.

Natalia slides in, sharing a conspiratorial look with Mariel before placing her folder beside the scattered plans. Ivy settles across from her, flipping her laptop open. The room settles. Lucien's voice is deliberate—almost too calm. His gaze moves from Marcus to the Brotherhood insider, then lingers on Mariel, as if weighing the measure of their faith.

"They'll sweep the fortress perimeter every thirty minutes with updated security signatures," Lucien says, gesturing at the blueprints. "Ivy, you'll have a six-minute window to black out their surveillance. We go in when their data resets." His tone bears the chill of a man who's lived with the cost of betrayal. "Natalia, you handle press comms and real-time code. No leaks, not even to Lauren."

Ivy's fingers brush the keys. The laptop's glow sharpens her jaw, turning her features angular. "I'll need deep access to the Brotherhood's internal firewall. I can mask our trail, but one echo on the wrong channel and their system will eat me alive." Her voice has an edge of defiance—next to Lucien's composure, it sparks, frantic.

Marcus cracks his knuckles, glancing at the insignia stitched on his sleeve. "I have people on standby near Fifth and Lex. But they still bleed Brotherhood green. If this goes sideways, I can't guarantee what they'll choose." His voice is soft, a warning barely above a murmur.

Mariel looks to Natalia, her posture taut as wire. "We can't do this halfway. Once it starts, there's no pulling back. If anyone's got doubts, now's the time." The words hang between them, a daring challenge.

Natalia's lips twitch, not quite a smile. "There's no one I'd rather risk this with." She raises her hand, palm open.

A sigh unravels in Lucien's chest. Every room like this, every hushed huddle before a storm—they blur together in his memory: men he trusted lost to bullet wounds and greed, plans shattered by whispered betrayals. The weight of those scars presses cold along his ribs, reminding him to watch, always, for the tremor of a hand or the side-eye of doubt.

Ivy silently nods, unplugging her headphones. She glances at Marcus, searching for an answer to a question they never voice.

Marcus rests a heavy hand on Mariel's shoulder. His touch is steady but hesitates at the edge of trust, as if he cannot help but remember the nights when loyalty meant nothing and survival meant everything. "If you run, you signal twice—nothing more. I'll cover it from the inside. You have my word."

Natalia sweeps burner phones across the table, sliding one to each ally. "Use coded phrases. If you hear anything about a 'midnight lantern,' that's your go-signal. Otherwise, radio silence."

In this room, glances replace handshakes, uncertainty threaded through every gesture—a quick exhale, the tightening of a jaw, the barely perceptible flex of Lucien's fingers over his own burner. Mariel brushes a stray curl behind her ear, her eyes never leaving Lucien, as if some private conversation is happening beneath the clatter.

"The last time I trusted someone," Lucien says quietly, so only Mariel hears, "I counted corpses before the sun came up."

She doesn't answer, but the line of her mouth softens, and for a second, there's understanding—a reconciliation of betrayals past and the peril ahead.

Lucien moves to the whiteboard, markers squealing as he scrawls escape routes, contingency codes, exit points. "If anything falls apart, you follow protocol Alpha. Don't wait on me. No one moves before the signal." The authority in his voice brooks no dissent, but he senses—subtle and sour—the questioning in the room. Not overt, never voiced; just the prickle of possibility that tonight, history could repeat i tself.

Shadows climb the damp walls as dusk thickens, swallowing words and lending the space a haunted, electric charge. Natalia clasps Ivy's hand. Marcus's gaze flickers to the other Brotherhood insider, a silent treaty forged in the old language of necessity.

"Let's do what we came to do," Marcus says at last.

Ivy tucks away her laptop, Natalia pockets her phone, and one by one, they slip into the city's dim corridors—each marked by purpose, carrying pieces of hope and dread.

The door swings shut behind the last ally. In the hush that settles, Lucien and Mariel are left staring at a jagged horizon through a fogged window, hearts beating out the count until morning.

Midnight Storm

The black car skids to a halt at the curb, sleek as a blade beneath the broken jaws of midnight thunderclouds. Lucien is the first out, his suit jacket plastered to his frame by wind and rain that bites, needling his skin with icy precision. Mariel stumbles after him, clutching the door, her hair already slicked to her cheeks. The city's noise recedes behind a ceaseless roar—rain pinging off glass and concrete, thunder cracking above so sharply that it vibrates in bone. Lightning throws the Brotherhood's fortress into jagged relief: brutal architecture hunched between glittering towers, stone dark as stormwater, with no sign or flag. Just the cold, silent promise of power.

Lucien scans the empty street. Manhole covers glimmer like eyes. A distant siren wails and dies. Somewhere, in another lifetime, the Orion Club's old guard might have laughed at the idea that anything could touch them. Now the air itself feels volatile, charged like gunpowder. He wraps an arm around Mariel, drawing her close as they push through a river of rain. Her breath hitches, shivering at the cold—or from the awareness of what waits inside. Their shoes slap and skid across pavement slick enough to swallow the unaware.

A faint glow above the concealed entry strip—no doormat, not even rust on the steel—guides Lucien. He flicks out his keycard. For a heartbeat, nothing happens. The magnetic lock hesitates, then relents with a sigh, and Lucien barrels them through before the storm can reconsider. They tumble into the antechamber: a cavern of shadow and humidity. Marble floors pool with runoff, echoing each drip and ragged exhale. Lucien's jaw tightens. Every fixture, every camera lens, is known to him—placed for control, now serving a threat unseen.

He shoves the heavy door closed with a wet arm. Mariel blinks against the sudden hush, rain still streaming down her face, her lashes clumped. Water beads along her collarbones. She exhales, a quick, shaking sound swallowed by the vastness of the room.

"You alright?" Lucien asks, his voice soft, pitched so it can't ricochet through the halls.

"Cold," Mariel answers, but she's already scanning the lines of security lights snaking overhead. Red diodes blink in a predictable pattern. She presses her fingers to her side, as if expecting the place to bite. Her gaze catches for an instant on a dark window opposite the foyer mirror—a prickle of movement—or imagination?

Lucien can almost feel the fortress breathe, old and heavy. Every inch is layered with contingencies: pressure plates buried in the floor beneath rugs, biometric locks disguised in antique paneling, concealed doors drilled through concrete like veins. Yet tonight, the certainty he's always held here—the sense that power, order, and history could keep chaos out—slips just beyond his reach. Paranoia isn't just prudent; it's all that's left.

They step deeper into the corridor, Lucien's hand hovering near his inner pocket. Mariel moves silently beside him, her shoes leaving damp, nervous prints. Each step is an invitation to memory: years spent chipping away weakness, building legend and paranoia brick by brick. Now, that work seems no more secure than a mask in a gale.

Somewhere above, boots click on tile. Lucien stills, motioning for Mariel to press back against the wall. Her eyes widen, every muscle drawn taut. On any other night, the fortress would swallow intruders whole. Tonight, it feels almost porous—too many doors, too many patched channels built by former architects eager for glory. He breathes deeply, steadying himself: this is his kingdom, fraught as it is, and tonight he must be both shield and sword.

The air sours with ozone, spiced faintly by the tang of old tobacco ground into the paneling. Another echo—the drag of a heavy heel, a mutter in a language Lucien learned only to break codes—and then nothing but the storm's drum far above. Even the blinking security lights seem jittery, chasing one another down the vaulted ceiling.

Suddenly, a hand closes on his sleeve. Mariel's grip is ice. Her other hand rises, palm trembling. "There—" she starts, but doesn't finish.

A siren erupts, splitting the silence, its blare so sinister that it vibrates in his molars. An emergency light ignites, crimson and pulsing, splashing horror across the corridor. Lucien's phone shrills with a burst of encrypted static. Breach: lower level. He reads it in code as if he's reading his own obituary.

Mariel flinches closer, pressed against him and the wall all at once. Shadows warp under the strobing pulse, deepening the hollow under Lucien's jaw, cutting Mariel's silhouette into sharp edges. The fortress bucks under thunder; somewhere, feet pound stone.

Lucien grabs Mariel's wrist, leading her—nearly carrying—down the corridor, senses drowning in iron and damp velvet. The alarm is relentless, mechanical and panicked, the pulse of an empire left unchecked.

They plunge into a shadowed alcove as armed enforcers storm past—faces half-lit and wild, guns raised, expressions caught between duty and fear. The red light turns sweat to blood on knuckles and flashes against the storm still howling beyond. The old stronghold, so long untouched, trembles. And Lucien, breathing the taste of challenge and dread, knows there's no more certainty left. Only what he can seize, heartbeat by heartbeat, with Mariel pressed close and every escape fading into chaos.

Lucien's hand tightens on Mariel's shoulder as they approach the central chamber. The storm's fury thrums through the bones of the fortress, muffled thunder rattling the stained glass in the vaulted ceiling overhead. Their footsteps echo on dark marble, each sound punctuated by the shrill alarm still pulsing through the hallways—a fevered warning that the old order is fracturing.

At the tall, iron-braced doors, Lucien hesitates just long enough for Mariel to sense the tension in his jaw. He pushes, shoulder set, muscles straining against centuries of weight, and the doors groan open. Floodlights scorch their vision white. Ahead, Brotherhood leaders cluster in a semicircle—trench coats damp from the leaking stone, guns glinting, eyes sharp with fear and betrayal. The scent of gun oil mingles with petrichor sneaking in from the rooftop vents.

Marcus Reed breaks from the line. He looks less like the implacable enforcer and more like a man at the edge of undoing, his gun trembling in hands roughened by too many nights spent beating back chaos. Lucien sees the flicker in Marcus's dark eyes—a plea, muted by suspicion and pain. The only sound is the scrape of Marcus's boots as he halts a stride from Lucien, tilting the muzzle just off center.

"You did this, Lucien," Marcus says, his voice low but raw. "You opened the gates. Set it all in motion. But you weren't alone, were you?" He jerks his head. "Natalia, tell them."

Lucien's breath hitches. Beside Marcus, Natalia Voss stands ghost-pale, rain matting her curls to her cheeks. Her hands twist in front of her, her silver nose ring flashing. Mariel's cry is sharp—wounded fury—her eyes luminous and wide with shock.

Natalia's lips tremble as she tries, and fails, to look at Mariel. "I didn't—" Her voice breaks, thin as wire. She turns, finally meeting Mariel's gaze, tears cutting lines down her face. "I was forced. They came after me, after you—Elias said he'd make you disappear unless I gave him what he wanted. I never meant—"

Shouted accusations split the air. The Brotherhood men surge forward, fury cresting. Echoes chase across marble and stone. Lucien's memories lurch—a different night, different betrayals—Celeste's haunted eyes, Elias's judging silence, the price he's paid for loyalty. Regret coils hot in his gut. He knows what it means to barter another's soul for a moment's safety. He knows, too, how that poison seeps between friends and warps everything it touches.

But guilt can't save them now.

He finds control—a cold clarity rising above his guilt—shoulders his way between the reeling adversaries, and triggers the device in his pocket. A low hum builds in the walls, then screens embedded high above the circle spark to life. For a heartbeat, everything is motionless. Then Mariel's files flicker across the glass—names, numbers, faces, secret ledgers, captured confessions. Shadows peel back, leaving rot exposed in the center of all that power.

Gasps echo. One of the older men staggers, muttering a prayer; another covers his mouth, eyes bulging at the raw, unfiltered truth. Even Marcus lowers his gun, uncertainty written in the set of his shoulders. Lucien watches all of it, dual threads tightening—his old allegiance unraveling, his resolve to shield Mariel hardening into something irreversible. Across the room, Mariel jams a flash drive into her phone with shaking hands, the blue glow reflected in the sheen of her tears.

"Enough!" Elias Kane, his silvering hair wild above blazing eyes, steps forward and lifts a pistol. The hush is immediate. "Loyalists—seize them. Now."

The chamber erupts. Lucien moves on instinct, slamming a guard's arm to the ground before the blow can fall. Mariel, bolder than anyone in the room, ducks beneath reaching arms and weapons and slams her thumb against her phone's screen. A digital howl splits the air—the Brotherhood's secrets are siphoned into the world, one damning document after another, broadcast to every glowing port and hungry news outlet.

Gunfire cracks—a wild note, echoing off stained glass. Lucien reels, his arm burning, but pulls Mariel close with his good hand. Her tears salt his suit; her whisper, close at his ear, is pure defiance and heartbreak. "With you. No matter what."

The room is chaos—Brotherhood men wrestling, some breaking for the exits, others frozen in horror. Natalia drops to her knees, her shoulders wracked with sobs; Marcus's gun hangs limp at his side.

It isn't the end, but Lucien knows something irreversible has begun. He presses his lips to Mariel's hair, a silent promise sealed as Ivy's remote hack slams the outer doors shut. Outside, police sirens rise, wailing higher than the fading storm.

Lucien and Mariel stand at the ruined eye of the conspiracy, battered and bound together, as old empires crack and the future—dangerous, uncharted—surges in.

Dawn gathers at the mangled heart of the fortress, catching on glass shards and blood-spattered marble like omens made flesh. The storm's violence has retreated, but the scent of gunpowder and sweat lingers beneath bright slashes of pink and gold that squeeze past the battered window shutters, painting long ribbons across the ruined floor. Mariel stands in the center of the chamber, grime streaked beneath her jaw, Lucien steady at her side—a battered pillar, his suit darkened with rain and something deeper. The hush in this space, broken only by the ragged breathing of the survivors, carries a weight more frightening than a thousand alarms.

Mariel inhales, her lungs aching with the aftermath—metal tang, smoke, and the distant trace of ozone. She finds her focus drifting over the chaos: toppled chairs, scorched tablets thrown aside in panic, and spatters of blood drying brown on ancient wood. Figures move in her periphery—the once-invincible architects of the Brotherhood now ghosted, haunted, uncertain which side claims them. She recognizes Marcus, his face drawn and bruised, Ivy awkward in her borrowed jacket, Natalia—Natalia, shoulders curled inward, eyes rimmed red above trembling hands. These were adversaries and strangers less than a night ago. Now, together they breathe the same air of ending and uneasy beginning.

Lucien's fingers close around hers, surprising in their warmth, their trembling. He leans closer, his voice pitched low for her alone, "We stood our ground. But the cost..." His gaze flicks over the carnage, the ruined sigil blazing on the chamber wall. "There's no going back, Mariel." Their joined hands ground her. Where fire once burned defiance, exhaustion and victory twine uncertainly in her chest—cold, hard fear diluted by what they've managed to survive.

Her mind catches on the cascade of betrayals and alliances—on her own hunger for truth and the price extracted for every scrap of it. She remembers her hope, naive and solitary, battered in newsroom corridors and in rain-soaked alleys beside Lucien's impossible shadow. There was suspicion there, once—thick as oil and twice as flammable—but their doubts had been burned away, night after brutal night, replaced with something leaner: the understanding of what it means to share risk, and to bleed for someone when escape means nothing without their hand in yours.

She steps forward, feeling eyes track her across the room. Her voice carries, raw but resolute. "None of us came through this whole. People we thought we knew—people we trusted—failed us, one by one. But what remains, what we are now, is built in the open. I won't hide the truth anymore. Neither will Lucien." The silence swells, alive with the memory of ancient oaths unraveling.

Natalia breaks from the knot of exiles, her skirts dragging through grime. Her lower lip quivers, but she stands tall when she meets Mariel's gaze. "I'm sorry. I didn't..." She swallows hard, tears cutting fresh channels through dust. "I'll make it right. I have to." Their hug is ragged but real—Mariel's battered hope knit by the knowledge that even broken loyalties can heal, eventually. Ivy gives a thumbs-up from across the chamber, her hard smile wiped away by relief.

Doors crack open at the far end. Detective Samuel Graves enters, surrounded by officers in midnight blue. He surveys the devastation, his face unreadable, though his steady eyes pause on Lucien, then Mariel. Lucien doesn't hesitate—he steps forward, produces a worn drive from his inside pocket, and presses it into Graves's waiting palm. "Everything," Lucien says. "The ledgers. The blackmail. The Brotherhood's reach." Graves nods, his mouth tight, reverent as if receiving a holy relic.

Mariel passes her own battered folder—sleek with secrets and sweat—into Graves's hand. "Run it with the others. Let the world see. No more shadows." Something subtle passes between the three of them: old codes exchanged for tentative trust.

"Can you protect them?" Mariel nods toward Marcus, Ivy, Natalia, and the dazed defectors at her back.

"I'll try, Dawson," Graves murmurs, his eyes sweeping the room's ghosts, "No one here's getting left behind."

As sunlight sharpens outside, faint echoes of chaos recede—the storm's tattoo replaced by the gentle tap of water in ruined guttering. Mariel glances at Lucien, finding his fortitude transformed by raw openness. She no longer sees a mask of charmed menace, but a man who has nearly lost everything, and still chooses to stand in the glow with her. She hears Marcus's steady voice—rumbling resolve—and Ivy's delight as firewalls crumble with a final keystroke. Natalia's apology, soft but unbreakable.

Outside, something stirs—shouts, footsteps, the city's day awakening. Mariel's gut tenses for what comes next, but Lucien's thumb sweeps her knuckles, a silent promise reminding her they are together in this new world. The door swings wide. Allies close ranks behind them. Pink-gold dawn spills out, gleaming on wet stones and battered f aces.

Lucien squeezes Mariel's hand, his voice soft against the hush. "Ready?"

Mariel faces the future—past fear, past betrayal, past the fortress's crumbling shadow. "With you," she breathes—not as a concession, but as an oath.

They step out into the light. Somewhere above, the first sirens echo distantly, while high on the old walls, a crow's wing glimmers black against the morning. In another city, a surgeon's hands shake as rain falls on a hospital rooftop, and a nurse wipes tears from her cheeks as she clocks in, not knowing yet how love will set her free.

But that is for another story.

Epilogue

The courtroom victory was his, but the silence afterward felt heavier than the gavel's fall. Lucien lingered by the window of his penthouse, glass of scotch in hand, watching Manhattan's midnight lights blur against the dark.

Caius's words from weeks ago echoed in his head: The Brotherhood protects its own—but only if we stay sharp.

He thought of Mariel asleep in the next room, her presence both an anchor and a risk. For the first time, he wasn't sure protection and loyalty could coexist.

The vibration of his phone cut through the quiet. A single message flashed across the screen:

Darius Hale. Emergency.

Lucien's jaw tightened. The Brotherhood's surgeon never called without reason—and when he did, it meant another storm was about to break.

Final Thoughts

When the final page turns, what lingers is not just the fire of desire or the sting of betrayal—it is the echo of hope.

Lucien Blackwell's journey is not simply about power meeting passion, or truth warring with deception. It is about the fragility of human hearts hidden behind walls of steel, and the audacity of love to break through when everything says it shouldn't.

To you, dear reader, who has carried Lucien and Mariel's story in your hands:
May their battles remind you that the strongest among us still bleed.
May their confessions remind you that silence is never the end.
And may their love remind you that even in the darkest hour, there is always a flicker of light waiting to be found.

But this is not the end.
The Brotherhood watches. The city shifts.
And in the shadows of tomorrow, other hearts wait to be tested—other stories ache to be told.

Stay with us. The midnight has only begun.

Review Request

LOVED the Orion Dynasty Book Series?

Click here to leave your review on Amazon.

Your review helps this dark billionaire romance world reach new readers who crave power, passion, and redemption.

Or type this link into your browser:
https://www.amazon.com/review/create-review?asin=B0FSHH76SZ